DATE DUE
Fecha Para Retornar

TAKING LIBERTY

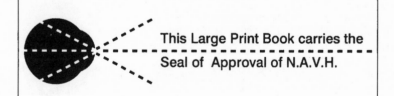

This Large Print Book carries the
Seal of Approval of N.A.V.H.

TAKING LIBERTY

The Story of Oney Judge,
George Washington's Runaway Slave

ANN RINALDI

Thorndike Press • Waterville, Maine

Published in 2003 by arrangement with Simon & Schuster Children's Publishing Division.

Thorndike Press® Large Print Young Adult Series.

The tree indicium is a trademark of Thorndike Press.

The text of this Large Print edition is unabridged.
Other aspects of the book may vary from the original edition.

Set in 16 pt. Plantin by Christina S. Huff.

Printed in the United States on permanent paper.

Library of Congress Cataloging-in-Publication Data

Rinaldi, Ann.
    Taking liberty : the story of Oney Judge, George Washington's runaway slave / Ann Rinaldi.
        p. cm.
    Originally published: New York : Simon Schuster Books for Young Readers, 2002.
    Summary: After serving Martha Washington loyally for twenty years, Oney Judge realizes that she is just a slave and must decide if she will run away to find true freedom.
    ISBN 0-7862-5557-9 (lg. print : hc : alk. paper)
    1. Large type books.   2. Judge, Oney — Juvenile fiction. 3. Washington, George, 1732–1799 — Family — Juvenile fiction. [1. Judge, Oney — Fiction. 2. Washington, George, 1732–1799 — Family — Fiction. 3. Slavery — Fiction. 4. African Americans — Fiction. 5. Large type books.] I. Title.
PZ7.R459Tak 2003
  [Fic]—dc21   2003049776

For the ladies of Mount Vernon
for their patience and assistance

PROLOGUE
February 1845
Greenland, New Hampshire

"So, Mr. Reporter, you say you write for the *Liberator*, do you? Well, and now it's a fine newspaper. Been around for a time now."

"Fourteen years, ma'am."

"And so, what can I do for you?"

"I'd like to do an article, ma'am. On you."

"Me? Posh, as Lady Washington used to say. An old lady like me? Haven't you reporters got anything better to write about? I'm seventy-three years old, young man."

"Yes. And that's why we want to interview you. You've seen a lot, done a lot. And you lived with the Washingtons as a child. Is that correct?"

"Lived with them? Yes, I suppose you could say that. Until I was twenty-four years old, I lived with them. I was Lady Washington's personal servant and companion until I left their employ. I was her favorite among the slaves at Mount Vernon since I was ten."

"And so can you tell us about them? What

it was like living at Mount Vernon? And New York, when he was president there? And Philadelphia?"

"I suppose I could."

"And you could tell us too why you left. We'd like to have the article in the paper for the president's birthday at the end of the month."

"I could. But there are other people still alive who can tell you too. George Washington Parke Custis, for instance. The general's stepgrandson. We used to call him Wash. He lives at a place called Arlington near the new federal city of Washington. Married Mary Lee Fitzhugh. Their only surviving daughter is married. A soldier man name of Robert E. Lee."

"You keep up with things, then."

"Oh, yes. I keep up with things, Mr. Reporter. Then there's Nelly Custis. She's the general's stepgranddaughter. Still living."

"We want to talk with you, Mrs. Staines. We're the *Liberator*, the abolitionist newspaper. We speak for people of color. And women. We want to know what it was like to be a slave of General and Mrs. Washington's."

"I had a life of comparative ease and even luxury."

"But you ran away."

8

"Yes, I did. And my life as a free woman was much harder to bear than it would have been if I stayed."

"Are you sorry you left, then?"

"Sorry? No, Mr. Reporter. Is a caterpillar sorry it becomes a butterfly?"

"That's the story as I see it, Mrs. Staines. Would you tell it to us?"

"Will you print it like I tell it?"

"I will."

"Then, sit down, Mr. Reporter. Sit down and listen."

CHAPTER ONE
1775
Mount Vernon, VA

One day when I was three, my mama took me by the hand and dragged me to the slope of lawn that ran down to the river in front of the mansion house.

It didn't even have the piazza on yet. There was lumber and stone to one end, and builders working. She put her hand on the back of my neck, the way you hold a chicken just before you're about to chop its head off.

"You see that house, Oney Judge?" she said to me. "Do you?"

Well, I saw it, all right. For me and all the other little children on the place it was always in our line of sight. Like the Throne of Grace the mistress was always reading about in her Bible. We couldn't help but see it. It was there when you woke up at dayclean, and in the night you could see it in the mists from the quarters, candles glowing in the long windows.

"Yes, Mama," I said.

"Well, you just take a good look, Oney Judge. 'Cause that house is where you gonna work when you get old 'nuf. You ain't gonna be no hoe Negra. You gonna be a fine mistress of the needle, workin' in that house for the mistress. Like your aunt Myrtilla do. And me. And Charlotte. And that's why I want you inside now, plyin' your needle, and not in the quarters listenin' to those tall stories that old no-'count Sambo Anderson be tellin' you."

"He tells me about Africa, Mama."

She hit me in the ear. "You doan need to know 'bout Africa. You here, not there. And if'n you doan wanna spend your grown-up days trudgin' in the hot sun and pullin' weeds all summer, you best listen. You hear?"

All I heard was a ringing in my ear. But she was mouthing more words, and I knew they weren't good. And if I didn't say yes, I'd get another hit in my other ear. So I nodded my head yes. And I promised I would practice my stitching. And she walked around to the back of the house to go in and have her morning time of sewing with the mistress and my aunt Myrtilla and Charlotte. Because they were all mistresses of their needles.

11

Other things about my first years on the place I disremember. But I know of those things. I suspect I was told them by Aunt Myrtilla.

Some was told by old no-'count Sambo Anderson, who hunted and trapped and wore gold rings in his ears and adorned his face with tribal scars and tattoos and was anything but no-'count to me and the other children. Because he was a saltwater Negro, come from Africa, he had great esteem on the place. So that everyone, Negro and white alike, listened when he spoke.

Some things were told to me by One-Handed Charles, who could salt fish better than anybody with two hands. Some by Nathan, who worked in the mansion kitchen with Hercules, the cook. And some by Lame Alice, who mended the fishing nets.

It was Nathan who told me the business of "first and second mourning."

It seems I had practiced with my needle enough to be allowed in the mistress's bedchamber early of a morning with Mama and Aunt Myrtilla and Charlotte. This was a privilege given to few Negro women. All Negroes who worked in the house had to be not only the best at their chores, they had to

12

be mulatto. Which, I soon learned, meant half white.

I was half white because of my daddy. He came from England. All'st he ever talked about was England. One time I heard him telling my mama about a place called Newgate. I thought my daddy was a squire, like the Fairfaxes, who lived next door. They came from England and they were fancified gentlemen.

I thought Newgate was his estate. And that someday he would take me and Mama there.

But when you play with other children, be they Negro or white, they soon set things right.

"Newgate is a prison," the other Negro children told me. "And your daddy's a convict. Our mamas say he was saved from hangin' by bein' sent to Virginia."

"Leastwise I know who my daddy is!" I shouted back. And Mama slapped me then, too. It didn't take much vexation for Mama to slap me.

"Is my daddy a convict?" I asked her.

"He's an indentured servant," she said.

It was early in the morning in the mistress's bedchamber. We hadn't had breakfast yet. And from belowstairs I could smell ham and coffee, and my stomach growled like the big, fluffy dog Sambo Anderson hunted with. The mistress's day started at seven because when her husband was home, he got up at four, made his own fire, wrote letters, then ate hoecakes and honey with her.

The mistress was belowstairs, seeing to the makings of dinner. Seems all they did was think about food in that house. The general and his lady had a regular fixation about food.

Winter sunshine poured in the windows. A fire burned in the hearth. Builders hammered away, making the south side of the house straight and true, the way the master said the corners of a house should be.

I sat on a rug trying to stitch the hem of a pillowcase.

"Mama, why do everybody in this house wear black all the time?" I asked.

"Doan ask so many questions," Mama snapped.

"But I like colors," I said. "Like the red of your head scarf and the amber beads the mistress sometimes wears. And the blue tea set she keeps on the sideboard."

"They all be in second mourning," Aunt Myrtilla answered.

Now, here was something. I stopped sewing. I liked morning, especially ones like this, when we came to the mansion house. I knew that soon Nathan would be bringing up a tray of food from the kitchen. Good food. Real coffee and fresh-baked bread and maybe some slices of ham. We didn't get much ham. Maybe some backbone, liver, what we called lights and whites called lungs. "Why do white folks get a second morning and we get only one?" I asked.

"Hush with your endless questions, child," Mama scolded.

At that moment Nathan came into the room. "Mistress send you all up some vittles." He set a tray of coffee, bread, butter, and ham on a table. Before he left, he squatted down beside me. Nathan was young, with bright eyes and short, fuzzy hair. Sometimes, when important company came, he got to wear livery. I knew what that was cause my Mama had helped sew it.

"There be two meanings to 'morning,' " he said. "One means 'the start of the day.' Like now. The other means 'a time of grief.' You grieve for somebody who died."

"Who died?" I asked.

He lowered his voice. "Lady Washington's daughter, Patsy. Last year. Got up from the dinner table in good spirits and fell on the floor in fits. In two minutes she wuz dead."

"What's fits?"

"It's what little girls get when they ask too many questions," Mama said.

"Daddy says it's the only way I'll learn."

"Your daddy puttin' notions in your head." Mama always said that.

"Your mama made the first-mourning dress for Lady Washington," Aunt Myrtilla explained. "Stayed up all night makin' it. Gen'l give her five shillings for her work."

I knew that Negro servants often got shillings or pence for doing special work. I couldn't wait until I was old enough to earn such.

"This second-mourning dress she wearin' now come from Richmond," Charlotte put in. "It wuz too long. Your mama fixed it. It gots a white collar. A little white allowed in second mourning."

"What about red?" I asked.

"No red allowed," Mama said.

"I see Master Jackie wearing a red vest under his black coat sometimes."

"You hush 'bout Master Jackie," Mama scolded. "Master Jackie does as he pleases. Doan need to 'splain to a little Negro girl what he do."

Master Jackie was dead Patsy's brother. Both were children from Lady Washington's first marriage.

"I like Master Jackie a lot," I said. "The

16

way he come to our house sometimes and give me sweetmeats. The way he always find Mama in this house and ask her to sew a button on his vest. 'Member, Mama? Master Jackie come one time when he was in trouble in school? An' you were sad 'cause Daddy was away?"

"You hush 'bout that!" Mama snapped.

I hushed.

"You come on down to the kitchen with me now, honey," Nathan said. "And I'll give you a sweetmeat." He reached out his hand. He was favored because of the way he could make rock candy. In the kitchen he had a teakwood barrel full of long strings of glistening rock candy. And he used it to make rich brandy sauces for plum puddings.

"Miss Patsy die of the falling sickness," he told me on the way down. "Dr. Craik give her mercurial tablets, but they do no good. No more talk 'bout dyin', now. You can watch me ready a pair of ducks. Lady Washington says they must be laid by, in case of company."

"I'm afeared of Hercules," I said. Hercules was head cook, small, wiry, and full of moods. He threw pots and pans when things didn't go to his liking.

"Hercules not gonna hurt a pretty little

girl like you. An' you listen, now, you're smart, too. Doan you ever stop askin' questions."

In the first years of my life I was happy. I lived in the two-story wood building on the service lane, north of the mansion. House families lived there. We had two chimneys, glazed windows, and finer blankets than those who didn't work in the house.

I was one of twenty-six children who belonged to women working at the mansion house, and I knew that house families were favored.

I knew my mama was favored. Everyone spoke good words about her round, pretty face. My daddy said she was taken with vanity, and it would bring her to trouble someday.

The first years of my life I took comfort and hope from the ordered world I lived in. And other than having to ply the needle, I could do as I pleased.

I and the other children would watch the builders working on the south end of the house, climb on the new lumber, hide in the quarry stone, until Mr. Lund Washington chased us away.

Mr. Lund, as we called him, was the general's kin. And he ran the place after the

18

general went to war. He was strict, but I soon learned how to bring him around. When it was hot, I'd fetch a glass of lemonade for him from the kitchen. When it was cold, I'd bring hot coffee. Sometimes he let me go out on the river on the schooner that Father Jack, Sam, and Schomberg used to fish for shad or herring. Once he held me high up in his arms so I could see the cupola they were putting on the red-shingled roof. It was the highest point I could see. And I just knew it pointed to heaven.

But I was only three and a half. And too smart, Mama said, for my own good. "You gets that from your daddy. He may be bound to Mr. Washington, jus' like a slave, but leastways he kin be free someday. Me never, an' not you, either. So you best learn to sit on all those notions."

I did not want to sit on my notions. I was determined that no one would make me afraid.

CHAPTER TWO

I continued to ask questions. There was much chance to learn and lots of people to learn from.

Servants gossiped. They had nothing else to do while they mended, chopped, spun, wove, dipped candles, plucked chickens, and ground wheat.

Servants (they were never called slaves) were close to everyone at the mansion house. They changed linens, washed them, emptied slops, knew who was sick and why, heard fevered mutterings and whispered prayers. They held secrets.

Nathan told me how the general had fought the French when he was a young man in the war. How he fought for the British. And now he was fighting against the British. I minded his words. I wanted to keep it all straight.

Nathan told me how the Fairfaxes, who lived in the plantation house next to ours, had been friends of the general since he was a boy. And they'd gone back to England because of the war.

He told me how the general's father had died when the general was eleven, and his older brother, Lawrence, took him under his wing. I couldn't believe the general had an older brother, because I thought the general was God. But then Nathan told me that Lawrence, the older brother, was dead, which I supposed allowed the general to be God.

He told me how this place known as Mount Vernon was once named Epsewasson, or Little Hunting Creek, by the Indians. That the Potomac was an Indian name too. It means River of Swans.

But Sambo Anderson told me about Africa.

I loved to visit Sambo. He raised lots of chickens that he sold to the mansion house. And his hunting dog could rout out grouse, partridge, ducks.

Most of the children were scared of Sambo. On his brown face strange markings were cut in. He wore rings in his ears, an owl's claw around his neck.

On a winter morning he sat outside his rude log hut polishing his old British musket that he hunted with. A small fire burned in front of him. On a spit over it he was roasting a rabbit. A muddy-colored blanket was draped around his shoulders.

"Sambo, I come to give you some biscuits from the house."

He nodded. "Little girl like you shud'na be out in the cole."

"Did you hunt last night?"

He nodded yes and pointed to the fowl hanging from a pole. He would sell it to Lady Washington. She counted on his bounty to dress up her table. He liked to hunt at night, like the owl that guided him. Said he could see better at night. I believed him.

I sat near the fire. "Tell me about Africa," I said.

I knew what would come first. I had heard it all before. The tribes. The way he said their names was like the sound of rain pattering softly on the roof. "Whydahs, Asante, Fanti, Ibo, Coromantee, Ga, Hausa," he said softly. And I waited for more.

"Vanished, all vanished," he said.

"What does that mean, Sambo?"

"Gone. From the Senegal River to the Congo, half a land away. Hausa lay in ambush, waited to capture Asante. Malinke went to war to capture Coromantee. Old, beautiful Africa puke up its own and sell them for slaves.

"Hausa make war on my people. Burn my village, kill my father. I was bound and sold for one hundred and seventy-two cowrie shells. Tied to others by a leather thong around my neck, marched for days to the sea."

I waited.

"My father was Asante king. They burned our village." He sighed and shook his head. "Now I am one of the Gone."

Then he fell into silence. There would be no more today. You couldn't push Sambo. "Tell me how it was when the general went to the Congress," I begged. Lady Washington had told us, but I liked the way Sambo told it better.

He shrugged and humphed. "Candles burn all night in the windows of the mansion house. People come and go. It wuz summer. News from the north bad, news from the south bad. Shadows on the bowlin' green. Paris an' Giles an' Joe from the stables hold the horse's reins. Gen'l's horse paw the ground, like he know sumptin' nobody else do. Heat lightnin' flash, like it did the night they burn my village. Bad sign. Finally outta the mansion house come the gen'l and that Henry man."

Patrick Henry. Yes. My daddy talked about that man. My daddy liked the way Mr. Henry talked about liberty.

"An' another man name of Pendleton. They come to ride off wif the gen'l. The gen'l's lady come outta the house an' watch 'em mount up. Then Billy Lee come from the stables all cocky like, 'cause he ridin' wif the gen'l to Philadelphia."

"And when he went to war?" I pushed.

"It wuz April. Whitefish runnin', we wuz plantin' corn. The gen'l's fish schooner on the river. The herring runnin' good. A rider come up the lane from Johnson's Ferry, like the devil be chasin' him. We Negroes all gather round and hear that up north they have a fight outsida Boston. The gen'l all excited. Everybody all excited. You never seed so many visitors as he had here then. This time he gather us round, tells us to work hard. Tells us he could lose everythin', could be taken away in chains, but he goin' to fight. He go off in the old green carriage wif that Mr. Lee and Mr. Carter. Say he be back in July. Well, he ain't come back yet. An' the old green carriage fetched home by Mr. Lund."

Sambo chuckled. "These white people doan know 'bout war. Ride off like gentlemans, wif lace at their necks, to meet and

24

talk. All they do is talk. They doan know how quick you can be one of the Gone."

Aunt Myrtilla came walking down the path in the quarters, a shawl wrapped tightly around her, calling my name. "Oney? Oney Judge, where you be? Your mama want you now!"

Sambo nodded at me. I set down the biscuits from the kitchen and left.

I ran about freely with the other children. To Dogue Run Farm, Muddy Hole Farm. The general had five farms altogether.

Mama didn't like my going to Dogue Run. She knew the general wanted his people to be Christian. She didn't want me learning the old ways, because my future was in the mansion house.

At Dogue Run they had Reverend Will, who practiced the old African religion, besides preaching about Jesus. On Dogue Run the slaves had night meetings in the gullies, and for those meetings Reverend Will was the keeper of the washpot. At night meetings they turned the pot over so the sound of their secret prayers would go under it.

And Dogue Run had old Sinda, who conjured.

Sinda was another saltwater Negro. Born in Africa, like Sambo. We children loved to

25

visit her. She could read the insides of a chicken to tell the future. She could make conjure bags out of red flannel, filled with ground-up toads' heads and goofer dust, which was graveyard dirt. She had a conch shell she said she had brought with her from Africa. "Water bring us here, water take us home," she'd said.

She told us never to let anyone get a piece of our hair.

"De hair is de most powerful thing your enemy kin git hold of," she said as we gathered around her. "It grow near de brain, an' anybody what git hold of it kin make your brain crazy."

She told us that if the general and Lady Washington had let her put a "fix" on Patsy, she would not have died. "Dat Patsy girl go crazy," she said. "She got fits 'cause spiders walk up an' down in her body. I cudda helped her. But no, dey doan want Old Sinda near de big house. Dat Patsy girl, she die 'cause of some sin her father do."

I made the mistake of telling Mama this, and she switched me. "That Mr. Custis, Patsy's daddy, was quality," she said. "An' you doan ever say such! An' you stay away from Dogue Run!"

But I still sneaked away and visited Old Sinda.

26

I recollect the way Sinda looked at me one day when I visited.

"Dis chile gonna be free one day," she said. "Dis chile gonna have trials, but she gonna be free."

I shivered. Did it mean my daddy would take me with him, when he was no longer bound to the Washingtons? But I soon put the thought in the back of my mind.

It was One-Handed Charles who told me how Master Jackie came to Dogue Run one day to ask Old Sinda to conjure for him. One-Handed Charles liked to brag that he was the last slave the general purchased. "In '72. From Mr. Massey. I come fer only thirty pounds 'cause I gots only one hand."

"But why did Master Jackie want Old Sinda to conjure?" I asked. "He has everything he wants at the mansion house."

" 'Cause he be wantin' to git betrothed to Miss Nelly Calvert. He wuz only eighteen. She wuz sixteen, and there wuz carryin' on at the mansion house fer days when he told his stepfather, the gen'l, he want to leave school. Everybody knew to stay clear. Master Jackie come beggin' Old Sinda fer some hush water in a jug, so he could give it to the gen'l to drink and quiet him down."

"What's hush water?"

"Jus' plain water what they fix so if you drink it, you be nice."

"But everybody knows conjure doesn't work on white people," I argued.

One-Handed Charles shook his head. "That still up fer speculation. Old Sinda give Master Jackie powders an' charms in a bag to put under the gen'l's bed."

"Did it work?"

"Is Master Jackie wed to Miss Nelly Calvert?"

"Yes."

"The gen'l come ridin' over here when he find out Master Jackie visit. Say nuthin' 'bout conjure. Complained that the carrots wuz too thin that year, the timothy not good 'nuf. He in a temper, all right. But Master Jackie, he git wed come February."

This was how I learned about life around me, the past of both the whites and the Negroes.

It all became my past. Sometimes I mixed up people in Virginia society with African tribes. When there was fear, after the general left, that the British would come up the Potomac and seize Lady Washington and burn the place, I saw in my head Sambo Anderson's village burned by the Hausa tribe. I saw Lady Washington with a leather thong around her neck, marched for miles to the sea.

My nightmares were about the general's horse pawing the ground, heat lightning flashing overhead, and Patsy rolling on the floor in fits because spiders were crawling up and down inside her body.

When you learn about someone, hear their stories, you tote them around. They flow in your blood and your dreams. They become a part of you. So that when something bad happens to you, there is something to liken it to. I know someone else it happened to. And he still lives and breathes.

So, when I was four and my daddy left, I cried, but I understood.

He became part of the Gone.

CHAPTER THREE

It was all Patrick Henry's fault that my daddy left. That's what my mama said.

"Your daddy been talkin' on 'bout that liberty thing since that fool Henry did his speechifyin'," she said. "That fool man shudda stuck to story-tellin' and lawyerin'. From what I hears, it's all the same thing anyways."

Lady Washington had told us about Mr. Henry of Hanover County. He'd done some fancy speechifying in Richmond before the war that made some people faint. " 'Give me liberty, or give me death,' " Lady Washington would whisper to us in the genteel quiet of her bedroom.

It sounded wonderful in there, with the fire crackling and us sewing. It didn't sound so wonderful in our dwelling when Daddy told Mama he was taking his liberty and leaving.

"It's fine and dandy for a storyteller from Hanover County to talk 'bout liberty," my mama said, slamming down our chipped cups on our chipped table. "But what happens to me an' little Oney when you leave us?"

"Mr. Henry was in the House of Burgesses," Daddy corrected her.

"I doan care what house he wuz in. Likely it wuz better'n this!"

"You know I can't take you," Daddy answered. "You always knew that, Betsy."

"Then why you hafta go?"

" 'Cause my indenture is up. I can work for my own now. Go west. Save money and buy your freedom. And Oney's."

"Why can't you work here?"

Daddy shook his head. "And be what? An overseer? All the white overseers end up drunkards. You see that big house up there on the hill and you think 'Why should I try? I ain't never gonna have anything like that. And if I fail, he'll take care of me.' No, I gotta leave here, Betsy. I gotta find my own way, even if it's not so easy."

"Well, you go, then! You just go!" And Mama threw a chipped cup across the room at Daddy.

"I'll be back," Daddy said. Then he kissed me and told me to be a good girl and practice my sewing so I could have a good place in the mansion house. And he walked

31

out the door. And became one of the Gone.

I wished I were older. There were so many things I didn't understand. I knew the West was over the Shenandoah, where Lady Washington said her husband had been when he was but a boy. Weren't there Indians in the West? I wondered why Mama cried so. Didn't she hear what Mr. Henry had said? You got liberty or death. Did she want my daddy to stay and die?

And hadn't Old Sinda said I would be free someday? Surely that meant Daddy would come back for us, didn't it?

Mr. Lund was in his mid years, a somber, sad man who became sadder after the general left. The general and Lady Washington trusted him with everything. He was not given to drinking. The general could not abide a man who drank.

During the war he had good reason to be sad. We had some bad times of it on the plantation.

That first year all Mr. Lund worried about was getting Lady Washington to leave too. That's what Mama told me. When Lady Washington was in her bedroom sewing one morning, he came to the doorway.

"Ma'am?"

"Yes, Lund."

"I've a letter from the general, ma'am. He has anxious thoughts for you. He asked if I could build a kitchen onto the townhouse in Alexandria."

"No need for a kitchen. I'll not be moving there." Lady Washington kept on sewing. "I do not spread myself far from this place, Lund."

"Lord Dunmore will be sending schooners up the river. Think of the position he could put your husband in if he kidnapped you!"

"Posh. What do they want with me, Lund?"

"Just the same, ma'am, I think it's time to lock away some of your husband's papers."

"I can help you with that, Lund. I'll gather them this afternoon."

Mama said she saw Lady Washington help him lock the papers away in the general's desk, saw her give him the key. Heard him say he'd never open it, lessen the general was there.

Another time he stood in the doorway of the bedroom: "I don't know what to do with the two hundred and forty-seven barrels of salt pork and beef laid by for the winter, ma'am. Nobody here to eat it."

Lady Washington sighed. "Jackie and his wife are coming to stay, Lund. And I'm sure there will be plenty of young people about then. Now, is there anything else?"

"No, ma'am. 'Ceptin, I'd like to get that little one there to spinning with the other little ones. At first I thought it wouldn't be worth the trouble. They'd be underfoot. And mess up the wool. But they're doing fine, and I could sure use that little one there."

He looked at me. I remember it good. Nobody had to tell me about it.

"This one?" Lady Washington put her hand on my head. "Why, she's just a baby yet. Give her time to be a child."

"With all respect, ma'am, it's wartime. And we need cloth to clothe the Negroes."

"This one you shall not have, Lund. She is my little pet. I intend to make her part of my household."

I felt a warm glow. From across the room Mama beamed at me.

Lady Washington left in the old green carriage in November for up north to be with her husband in the land of Massachusetts. Jackie and Nelly went with her. But I was kept in the house, to work, as she had ordered. The seamstresses were told to make a number of things: Shirts for the general when he came home. A new waistcoat. A gown for her. One for Nelly.

We didn't use Lady Washington's room. That summer we sat in the brick-floored kitchen, out of the way of Hercules.

In late summer Mr. Lund set us to gathering corn and putting it in baskets. And he read us a letter from the general:

" 'Let the hospitality of the house, with respect to the poor, be kept up. Let no one go hungry away. If any of these kind of people should be in want of corn, supply their necessities.' "

Mama and I and Aunt Myrtilla were in charge of the corn. And people did come, people fleeing Norfolk when Dunmore shelled and burned it. And then again, later, when the women and children left Alexandria to get out of reach of the enemy's cannon.

They came by in carts, wagons, moving their goods. They came up the road to Mount Vernon. And none went hungry away.

But there was trouble that summer and fall. The new chimney in the new room smoked every time the hearth was lit. It blackened the walls and they had to be repainted.

Mr. Lund fought all the time with Mr. Lanphier, the head builder. "If there is anyone more worthless in this world, I cannot think of him," he said.

One day Mr. Lund came upon us sewing in the kitchen and gave orders: "Five ships have been sighted at the mouth of the Cone River. We're gathering up the general's china, glass, and silver and putting them into barrels and casks and trunks. I need you all to help. Come along."

All morning we worked in the dining room, packing things away. Outside it was a hot September day. Around noon, as the last of the barrels was being loaded into a wagon to be taken to a neighbor's barn, Lame Alice, who walked with a cane, came shuffling across the bowling green in back of the house.

"Mr. Lund, Mr. Lund, come quick. James the cooper, he done drowned in the millrace."

We all went running. We children swam a lot on the edges of the Potomac, down by the wharf, when it was hot. We didn't swim in the millrace. Mama had told me you could not trust the water. "It has tricks in it," she said. "When the mill ain't runnin', there be no current. You can't see how deep it be."

When we got there, Paris and Giles from the stables were pulling James's body out.

"You children get away from heah!" Mr. Lund ordered.

There were about a dozen children gathered around now. We backed off, then crept up again to see the dead man.

"What happened?" Mr. Lund asked, kneeling besides James.

"We wuz ditchin' the swamp, like you tol' us this morning," one of the laborers, named Davis, said. "When we stopped to eat, James stripped and went in."

"He couldn't swim," Mr. Lund argued. "He was afraid of water."

"He wuz gonna go in jus' to his waist." Davis gasped and wiped a hand across his eye. "Afore we know it, he under."

"It's near eight feet in some places!" Mr. Lund stood up and looked around, seeking an answer. All he saw were stricken Negro faces.

And Old Sinda.

She stood on the other side of the mill-race, hissing. "Carpenter James cut his foot wif his own ax dis mornin', Cooper James drown. Miller Roberts at Dogue Run, drunk all de time. Wind last night break de corn off below de ears. Next thing you have a blight on de wheat. You ain't got 'nuf salt. De people run mad wifout salt. An' de bull kill somebody soon. Best thing, you let Old Sinda come an' work a fix."

"Get her outa heah," Mr. Lund directed Davis. "Before I do something I'll be sorry for."

Old Sinda hissed again. "Next best thing, British come up de river and burn dis place. Let us all free."

"I said get her outa heah!" Mr. Lund yelled.

Davis ran around to the other side of the millrace, and Old Sinda moved off. But she called back over her shoulder, "I do a fix an' get you some salt. Den you believe Old Sinda."

Mr. Lund paid no mind. He was sick over James. "General not gonna like this," he mumbled. And he looked up the hill at the house, with its scaffolding, and fingered the sore on his lip. He scowled at us children. "I told you to get out of heah, didn't I?"

We ran.

What came out of the drowning of James were two things: Mama wouldn't let me swim in the river anymore. And Mr. Lund, who was all the time writing to the general, started reading us some parts of the general's letters, regular like.

No, three things. Because I couldn't swim in the river, I crept through the pasture where the bull was kept, to take a shortcut to a small stream on the other side of it. One day that September I left the pasture gate open.

The bull got out and gored the gray wagon horse to death in the yard. I remember running and screaming for Mama.

She came out of the kitchen with Aunt Myrtilla, and Sall and Caroline, the housemaids.

Just then Mr. McKnowles, the hired bricklayer, went after the bull to try to get him off the gray horse, who was making terrible screaming sounds.

The bull turned and charged Mr. McKnowles. Sall and Caroline slapped their aprons at him. Mama waved a broom.

The bull knocked down Mr. McKnowles and was pushing him on the dusty ground when Mr. Lund and Paris and Giles came running from the stables. Mr. Lund shot off a musket. Negroes came running from all over.

Mr. Lund made the frightened Negroes hold the bull down with ropes while he tried to saw off its horns. He couldn't do it and had to give up. He fastened a board across them.

"Mama," I told her later in the dark of our own house, "Old Sinda said the bull would kill somebody. I made it come true."

"You hush 'bout that," she whispered savagely. "An' you hush 'bout leavin' that gate open. Mr. Lund find out, he switch you good."

"Lady Washington said I was never to be switched."

"Well, she ain't here, is she?"

Mr. McKnowles was laid up, bad. They didn't think he would live. The horse died.

By the end of the week Conway's sloop came to Alexandria, being that there were no British tenders in the river. And Mr. Lund was able to buy salt. It cost him seven pounds a bushel.

But he let Old Sinda come to one of four new buildings near the main house, where Mr. McKnowles lay in a bed brought there for him. Old Sinda brought her remedies. But she was not allowed near the mansion house.

Mr. McKnowles did heal. Mr. Lund started talking about joining the army. "I don't need this vexation," I heard him say to Nathan in the kitchen a week later. "Webster is sick. Gunner is laid up with a sore foot, Jack is getting so crazy he scarce works two days a week. I think he has consumption. Old Peter and Schomberg are coughing their guts up. And I've got six Negroes over to Dogue Run with the ague. The army would be heaven compared with this."

Still, he didn't leave. He kept making us listen to parts of the letters from the general.

And that is how he made us part of the general's troubles. And how I learned about the progress of the war.

CHAPTER FOUR

What Old Sinda had said about the British coming and setting us all free was no trifling talk. And it was one of Mr. Lund's worst worries.

Even Mama began talking about it all the time, since my daddy left.

Liberty.

I paid no never mind. She was always talking about being free, especially when she was night-walking with some of the other women to the different plantations to visit friends.

The general allowed nightwalking. Mr. Lund did not like it. The Negroes went through the fields and woods at night carrying flaming torches. Some to visit husbands, wives, or children at other plantations. Some to catch up on what was happening in Alexandria. Some just to make mischief.

"One of these days they're gonna set the

woods or fields on fire," Mr. Lund grumbled. "And in the morning they're so spent, they can't work."

And then came Lord Dunmore's offer of freedom to any slave who joined the British forces.

I was old enough to understand what that meant. I heard the Negroes talking about it among themselves. I saw the look in Mama's eyes when she spoke of it to others.

I knew my mama's eyes. Sometimes she scrunched them up so you wouldn't know what she was thinking. When they looked like fish eyes, I knew to run. But when she talked about freedom, I looked in them and saw nothing.

My mama was already one of the Gone.

And I knew someday the rest of her would catch up to the nothing in her eyes when she spoke about liberty.

I heard Mr. Sears, the carpenter who was working on the dining-room chimneypiece, tell Mr. Lund: "You ask me, I'd say all these Negroes around here would go to the British if they had the chance. Any word from Humphries?"

Humphries was a painter, and an indentured servant, like my daddy had been. He'd run off to the British.

"No," I heard Mr. Lund say, "but I know

43

one thing. He comes here and endeavors to land at Mount Vernon and raise the Negroes to action, I'll shoot him. That will be some satisfaction."

Shoot him! I must tell Mama.

Before I got a chance to, Humphries came, that very night. But Mr. Lund never knew it.

I lay in my narrow bed in our part of the servants' house. I heard the baying of dogs, someone shushing them, footsteps in another part of the house, then a commotion. I got up.

In the kitchen candles burned, sending long shadows. There were Mama, Aunt Myrtilla, Nathan, Hercules, Sall, Caroline, and a white man, bedraggled and red faced.

"I just come to let you know. The British mean it. Freedom if we join them. You all been good to me when I was here workin'. I just want you to know."

"How do we find these British?" It was Mama.

"They be comin' up the river one of these days. Be ready."

Then there were shouts outside. More baying dogs. "Lund," I heard Mama say. Aunt Myrtilla shoved a sack of vittles into the man's hand.

"Take me wif you," Mama said.

44

In her eyes she was already Gone.

For a moment the man was stayed by Mama's thought. He looked about to say yes.

"What's wrong wif you?" Aunt Myrtilla stepped between Mama and Humphries. "You gots a little one here. You hush your mouth 'bout leavin'."

"I can't take anybody," Humphries said. "I'm on the run."

I ran and grabbed Mama's skirt. "Mama, I heard Mr. Lund say he'd shoot Humphries if he came around."

"You see that?" Aunt Myrtilla snapped. "You best go on now." She pushed him out the door.

The others agreed. "You see anythin' of my husband?" Mama called softly after him in the night.

From the dark came the answer: "Your husband's too smart to stay around here, Betsy. And you should be too."

As he'd turned to answer I saw his white face, anxious, in the dark. And I thought, *I know now why God made us black. So when we run, we can't be seen.*

Nobody had to tell me to keep a still tongue in my head about Humphries. I had learned to do that by now. And every day, it seemed, I had more reason.

One reason was learning to read.

Negro servants did not learn to read. There was no hard rule about it. It was just not done.

Lady Washington liked to read us the Bible while we sewed in her bedchamber. Sometimes she let me sit beside her and even turn the pages for her.

"You see?" she said to me one day before she left. "There is the name of Jesus."

I saw. And I learned to know it on the page. At first I couldn't believe that I could do this. It leaped out at me, every time. It was like a bell ringing, a fire alarm in the night.

Next thing you know, I'd pick up the Bible when Lady Washington left the room and run my fingers down the page looking for the name. And I'd flood with joy when I found it.

After she left for Massachusetts, I started looking around the mansion house for other things besides the Bible that had words written down.

I soon found what I wanted in the kitchen. One of Lady Washington's most prized possessions was her cookbook. It was large and bound in cloth.

I soon minded how Nathan and Hercules looked at it before they put salt or butter in a pot, before they cracked open eggs or parceled out spices.

It was a time of war. A time to be careful with food. There was not enough coffee, sugar, salt. Mr. Lund required an accounting of the usage of such.

"Follow the recipes," I heard Hercules tell Nathan. And then it came to me.

You couldn't follow all those recipes Lady Washington had if you couldn't read.

One day, when Aunt Myrtilla and Mama had left me alone in the kitchen stitching a hem, I asked Nathan about it.

"Come here, and I'll show you," he said.

He set me on a stool next to the large wooden table. And he ran his brown finger down the written words of the recipe. "What this says is, 'Take a pan of fine flour and rub into it half a pound of fresh butter.' See? This word is 'flour.' This is 'butter.' "

"And this?" I asked. " 'Egg whites.' "

"And this?"

" 'Melt butter.' "

"You mean from these words you make a cake?"

"Tha's right, baby. And all these recipes been handed down in Lady Washington's family. She's right proud of them."

"Can I learn the words, so someday I can make a cake?"

"You should learn your letters first," Nathan said.

At that moment Hercules turned around. He was a small man, wiry and quick to anger. "You watch yerself there, Nathan," he said in a warning voice.

"I'm watchin'," Nathan said.

"You do that an' you proddin' a hornet's nest with a stick."

"I ain't afraid of hornets," Nathan said.

"Well, you shud be."

Nathan shrugged and winked at me. "I'll show you how to make a cake, baby, but you gotta promise: You tell nobody about learnin' these recipes. You hear? Not even your mama."

I understood. One more thing I had to keep a still tongue in my head about. I understood something else, too. Both Nathan and Hercules could read.

And so I learned to make a cake. Or a Brunswick stew. Or blueberry grunt, or beefsteak and kidney pie, or trifle and rich custard.

I learned to know the words before I learned my letters.

One pint of berries.

Sprig of parsley.

Spoon of cinnamon.

I memorized the recipe for trifle and soon knew it, word by word.

" 'Put slices of Savoy cake or Naples biscuit at the bottom of a deep dish; wet with white wine and fill the dish nearly to the top with rich boiled custard; season half a pint of cream with white wine and sugar; whip to a froth — as it rises, take it lightly off and lay it on the custard pie; pile it up high and tastily, decorate it with preserves of any kind, cut so thin as not to bear the froth down by its weight.' "

The day I could read that I beamed at Nathan. "It's better than finding Jesus in the Bible."

"You not only breakin' the law," Hercules scolded him, "you're teachin' her blasphemy."

But Nathan was so proud of me he could bust. So we went on to the next recipe, beefsteak and kidney pie.

Nathan told my mama and Aunt Myrtilla he was teaching me to cook. And he was.

"Tha's good," Mama said. "She be sure of havin' a place in the house then." She never gave a thought to how you knew what went in the pot and how much. Nobody else in the mansion house did either. Likely not even Lady Washington.

The day I made my first pear pye, I was so

proud I thought I would bust. Nathan and Hercules let us eat it in the kitchen. We even gave a piece to Mr. Lund.

"Glad to see this little one is carryin' her weight," he said.

And I was more proud of myself than when I learned to find the name Jesus in the Bible.

CHAPTER FIVE
Fall 1776–Spring 1777

The general wanted trees planted in the fall.
Mr. Lund had his orders. " 'Plant trees in the
room of all dead ones in proper time this fall.
I mean to have groves of trees at each end of
the dwelling house. Locusts and all clever
kinds of trees, crabapple, poplar, dogwood,
sassafras, laurel, and willow, especially weeping willow, twigs of which may be got from
Philadelphia,' " he read to us.

The Negroes grumbled in great plenty.

"Some 'o dese trees not gonna live, Mr.
Lund."

"Why we gots to plant so many?"

"British only gonna come an burn everythin' down."

Mr. Lund silenced them. "Y'all listen up,"
he said. And from his pocket he withdrew
another letter, very rumpled. "I'm gonna
read y'all this. I shouldn't, but I'm gonna.
The general's been chased out of Long Island by the British."

And he read: " 'Such is my situation that if I were to wish the bitterest curse to an enemy this side of the grave, I should put him in my stead, with my feelings; and yet I do not know what plan of conduct to pursue.' "

"Y'all hear that?" Mr. Lund demanded. "The general's got enough trouble. So we're going to do what he asks so as not to give him anymore. Those trees he wants planted, we're gonna plant. And we're gonna plant 'em straight and true."

There was no more grumbling about trees.

Master Jackie came home with his wife Nelly, who was heavy with child. It was born at Mount Vernon, a girl they named Eliza. A baby in the house made for much running and fetching and fussing. Nelly stayed in bed for weeks, something I had never seen Negro women do.

Most of them were in the fields again the next day, or at their tasks.

Then Lady Washington came home in November. The house came alive again. Once more we had sewing in Lady Washington's bedroom. And she told us how she'd been in Philadelphia when the bells rang in July.

"They rang and rang for liberty," she said. "Oh, the joy went through my bones."

I saw the look on Mama's face and knew that something was going through her bones, all right. But it wasn't joy.

The house was soon filled with young people, and Mr. Lund grumbled. "I got twenty-four horses to feed in the stable. Master Jackie keeps seven, five for Mrs. Washington's chariot, seven mares, the wagon horses, and my one. Then the visitors come and we have to feed theirs. Where am I supposed to get all this corn?"

Another time he gathered us all together to read a letter he was writing to the general.

" 'Doll had a little one this fall. The children have spun enough thread to make a piece or two of linen, which we are preparing to have woven. We have nine wheels at work. Our little people are very dependable. Yes, the British came up the Potomac and burned Robert Brent's plantation, but they were driven off by Colonel Grayson's militia before effecting more damage. Jackie and Nelly arrived home safely.'

"We got to keep his spirits up," he told us. "The general has an army with no clothes, no food. He lost a battle in White Plains. New York City is lost. If he wants us to build another wing on the house, we'll do it."

At Christmastime another letter came, and Mr. Lund gathered us around to listen:

53

" 'If there can be any possible makeshift made, without buying cloth for the Negroes at the enormous price you speak of, it ought to be attempted. Without making the poor Negroes suffer too much. This I would not do to save any expense, as they certainly have a just claim to their victuals and clothes.' "

Then Mr. Lund raised his head from the letter and looked at us. "He's in Pennsylvania," he said. "Driven there by the British. His men scarce have any clothes. Some have no shoes on their feet. He thinks, right now, that he may lose the war and be taken in chains to England. But he thinks of you. And all he wants is to make sure you've got warm clothes."

Then he gave us presents. Rum and shoes to the men, rock candy and oranges Master Jackie had gotten off a ship in Alexandria to the children, blankets and new shifts to the women.

I helped Nathan smoke a pheasant for Christmas. I learned the words *brine* and *wood chips*. When Master Jackie heard I helped Hercules and Nathan, he came into the kitchen himself and gave me a shilling.

"Can you make buttermilk biscuits?" he asked me.

"No," I said, "but I can learn."

He knelt down beside me. "Tell you what, Oney. My mama favors you. And I can see why." He peered into my face. He tucked my hair behind my ear. "You're a pretty little girl, and Mama considers you one of the family. How would you like to rock little Eliza to sleep on occasion?"

I said I would. He gave me a hug. And so it came about that I went into the nursery twice a day to rock Eliza's cradle until she fell off to sleep.

It meant less time in the kitchen, but I still helped there every day too. I asked Nathan for the paper on which it was written about buttermilk biscuits.

I was learning to copy the scrawls about "beating well" and "making sure the oven is hot" and "kneading gently."

Nathan had given me a quill pen and some old parchment and ink.

Mama was furious when she found out.

"What you doin' there could get us all in trouble," she scolded. "You crazy, girl?"

"I'm only learning to be a good cook, so I can work someday in the kitchen for Lady Washington," I said.

Mama was torn between wanting to dash the bottle of ink on the floor and hoping I could learn everything.

"You hide that good when you finished,"

she said. "Mr. Lund find that paper and writin', and we be shipped off to the West Indies."

And she never said another word about it.

Mr. Lund kept us informed. The general would not be taken in chains to England. Not yet, anyway.

"He made an attack in a place called Trenton," he told us, "on Christmas night. He will be all right for a while."

When she came home again, Lady Washington insisted I be at her side when I was not rocking Eliza or working in the kitchen. "You are growing into a remarkable child," she told me one day. "You understand everything full well. You think like one of my own. How would you like to accompany me about while I take inventory of the pantry, the icehouse, the weaving house? Even the barnyard, where we'll see this spring how many new lambs we have?"

"Oh, I'd most admire to, ma'am," I said.

"Well then, we must see to it that you are dressed in a seemly manner." And immediately she began going through the yards of cloth she'd brought home from Philadelphia. The colors made my heart leap. Surely such colors had been squeezed out of the very flowers themselves!

"We'll have your mama stitch you a new petticoat and apron and chemise. Mayhap two," she said.

My mama, who wore homespun of a mud color and was still young and pretty, took on the task but grumbled at me quietly. "Doan you get any fancy notions 'cause you gonna get fine new feathers," she warned me. "You 'members your place."

I paid for those new clothes — to Mama. She slapped me more often. She called me "Lady Washington's brat" when I angered her. "You get ink on those clothes an' you'll have some 'splainin' to do," she warned.

In our servants' dwelling I wore my old clothing. I did get ink on my hands, learning to make my letters and words, and when I did, I spent many an hour in the washhouse, trying to wash it off.

All that spring I was at Lady Washington's side while she took her inventory. I held her cloth-covered account book and, on top of it, the little silver tray with the bottle of ink and her quill pen.

The general had written home: "How many lambs do you have this spring? How many colts have been born? Have you any prospect of getting paint and oyl? Are the covered walkways done?"

Mr. Lund must pen an answer. The general was in a place called Morristown in the land of New Jersey. Lady Washington was to join him soon.

So in the pasture Lady Washington counted the lambs and wrote it down in her cloth-covered book.

The book was set on the ground. "Two dozen," her writing said. I knew what a dozen was. Nathan had taught me to count eggs, and there were twelve eggs in a dozen.

I counted the lambs. "Ma'am?" I asked.

"Yes, Oney?"

"Is a dozen lambs the same as a dozen eggs?"

"Of course, child, why do you ask?"

"What you put in the book, ma'am, is two dozen. I count twenty-eight lambs."

She stared down at me. *Too late, too late,* I thought. Oh, and my heart fell inside me as I tried to meet her eyes.

"Oney, how do you know what I wrote in the book?"

The book lay open on the ground between us. "I just know," I whispered, dropping my gaze.

She knelt down beside me. "Oney Judge, you can read, can't you?" she asked gently. "And you can do sums."

I was fair trembling. Now I would be sent to the West Indies! Maybe my mama, too!

"Please, ma'am," I begged, "don't send my mama to the West Indies. Send me if you have to, but not my mama!"

I heard the rustling of her gown as she gathered me in her arms. I smelled the lavender water she wore. "How did you learn, Oney?" she asked. "I won't punish you. Or your mama. Tell me."

"I wanted to learn your recipes," I said. "The ones Nathan said were handed down in your family. You have to read to know the recipes."

"Ah," she said softly. "Yes. It is something most people don't realize. Not even the general. Well, I always said you were a bright little baggage. So, this will be our secret, then, won't it? We won't tell anyone. Will we?"

"No, ma'am."

"Not even the general when he comes home. He'll have so much on his mind anyway, he doesn't have to know. Does he?"

I breathed a sigh of relief. "No, ma'am."

As we walked back to the house she told me something then. "When I was a girl, Oney, and Mr. Custis was courting me, my father wouldn't hear of marriage to him. Why, his family did not even have a coat of arms and were too low in rank in Virginia society."

I was sure that Lady Washington's first husband, the father of Master Jackie, did not go without a coat on his arms in the winter. I listened.

"I was a Dandridge, you see, before I was a Custis or a Washington. That was my father's name."

"Like my daddy's name is Judge."

"Yes. Well, my father said he would throw the family silver and jewelry into the street before he would give them to a Custis. Do you know how I won him around to getting his blessing for my marriage?"

"No, ma'am."

"My father was living with a young Negro boy he'd taken in and treated like a son. I knew how much he loved that boy. So I presented the boy with a pony and a saddle. And I was good to him. So you see, I suppose I'm a little like my father after all. I have taken a great liking to you, and you are my special pet, and I shall always look after you."

I was taken with joy. "Yes, ma'am," I said. And from that moment on, I knew I would have died for Lady Washington if she'd asked me.

CHAPTER SIX

There was a quart of anger in my mama, not a pint, but a quart, which she sometimes whipped into a froth and threw at me. That is the only way I can tell it. In the words of Lady Washington's cookbook. To some it was a puzzlement, but I put it down to my daddy's leaving and all my new clothes.

She'd been made to sew those clothes for me, while she still wore what she likened to sackcloth.

Her anger was stirred up anew at me every day. She even quoted the Bible, something she did when it pleased her. "It doan give glory to the Lord. It's the puttin' on of gold and costly apparel," she said of my clothes. I don't think she even knew what that meant. Surely I didn't.

And to punish me: "We goin' to market tomorrow morning, so you git yourself to bed early tonight."

Mama often rose early of a Sunday to go

to market in Alexandria. The trip took two hours on horseback, up to three on foot. The general had always allowed this. Mr. Lund did not like it, but he could not take away the favor.

Mama made brooms to sell at market. And sometimes caps or aprons out of scraps of fabric she managed to "lay aside" after sewing.

She was always in great spirits when she came back from Alexandria. Always she had a shilling in hand and news of slaves on other plantations inside her head.

But she had never before asked me to go with her.

"I have to rock little Eliza for her morning nap," I told her. "I always do, for Miz Nelly."

"We be back by then," she promised. "An' if we ain't, let Mrs. Custis do her own rockin'."

I felt a sense of doom inside me. Abandon little Eliza? I liked caring for Eliza, knew I would be blamed for not being where I was supposed to be and could not go to Lady Washington, for she had left to join the general in the land of Morristown, New Jersey.

I woke before first light, in the cold and dark of the servants' quarters, and set out by foot to Alexandria.

Then, at the last minute, Jack the wagoner decided to come, so by turns we took rides in his wagon, getting in with the live chickens, Mama's brooms, caps, and aprons, two slaughtered sheep, tallow candles, linen, bushels of corn, and a goodly supply of twelve-penny nails. Mr. Lund was always bemoaning the disappearance of his twelve-penny nails.

I was cold and sleepy. Owls hooted around us, dogs bayed in the distance, and no candles burned yet in the houses we passed, though some Negroes came out from them to join us. All carried pine torches, and on the edges of the light they made, I could see bats flapping. Bats were the stuff of my nightmares. Old Sinda said they were a bad omen. I believed her.

The women brought along jugs of water. Some of the men had rum — stolen, most likely. A lot of stealing went on at the plantation. The general and his lady knew it.

The slaves stole what they could. Whatever they stole was owed to them, they said, and the general had plenty. They were always breaking into the meat house and making off with a leg of this or a haunch of that. Mr. Lund was always trying to secure the meat house.

We munched on roasted sweet potatoes.

There was much talk about joining the British. About how Master Jackie was so puffed up because he now "had a seat in the legislature."

I wondered why Master Jackie had to leave Mount Vernon to seat himself anywhere. They talked about Ariona, a child of Lame Alice's, being sick with worms. "She die soon," Mama said.

They talked about the French dentist who would be in town this day. "He givin' forty-two shillings fer a good tooth," one of the men said. Some of the Negroes spoke about selling their teeth. Mama was looking to purchase a small mirror for our part of the servants' quarters.

"You kin barter for that," Caroline told her.

"What I got to barter?" Mama asked. "I wants shillings fer my brooms. Maybe I barter a tooth."

"You're too pretty to do that," Charlotte advised. "You'll find somethin'." And then I became so tired Mama put me in the wagon, and I fell asleep and didn't hear anything else.

The Negroes were permitted to set up shop in Alexandria until nine in the morning of a Sunday. We arrived before six. Talk flew between Mount Vernon Negroes and those from other plantations. A Negro who had news was considered important.

Caroline told how Master Jackie's wife was with child again. Wagoner Jack said how Master Jackie was buying his own plantation near here.

A Negro woman named Sally who belonged to the Lewises told how her master, Fielding Lewis, was ailing. His wife was a sister of the general's.

Then, "You lookin' fer a nice dress, Betsy? Chloe, who works fer Mrs. MacIver, has a dress. Look 'bout your size. What you got to barter?"

Mama pulled me out from under the table. "You gon' do an errand for me," she said. "Why you think I brung you?"

She handed me three brooms and told me to go two tables down to Chloe, the Negro with the red turban, and give her the brooms for the dress.

I did so. The dress was quality, I could see that right off. It had a small red-and-blue design on cream-colored fabric and was folded neatly. I delivered it to Mama, who held it up against herself and sashayed about.

There were admiring glances from the women and hoots from some male Negroes, and Mama was pleased. By nine we were packing up for home.

"I's gonna wear this pretty dress tonight when I go nightwalkin'," Mama told me. "Now I be as pretty as you. 'Bout time, ain't it?"

"Yes, Mama." As soon as we got home I ran into the house to see to little Eliza.

I must have looked a sight. "Where you been?" Nathan asked.

"To town with Mama."

Miz Nelly found me in the downstairs hall. "Where were you this morning?" she asked. "And look at you. Your new petticoat and apron are filthy!"

I was hungry and spent. Tears rolled down my face. "I went to Alexandria with my mama."

"But you were supposed to mind little Eliza. You aren't going to be lax and un-trustworthy, are you, Oney?"

I knew what *trustworthy* meant. I did not know about the *un* part. And I did not know about *lax*. Was I lax? It sounded terrible. "Mama made me go," I said. "I'm sorry, Miz Nelly."

She sent me to the kitchen to eat. She made me wash and change before I touched little Eliza. And when I fell asleep on the floor in the baby's room after putting her down for the night, Miz Nelly covered me and let me stay right there.

So I was in the house the next morning when, first thing, Mr. MacIver came to the door and said he wanted his wife's stolen dress back.

Master Jackie invited him in. I hovered in the central passage of the house, listening. The name MacIver went through me like a chill. It was Mrs. MacIver's Negro servant Chloe that I'd gotten Mama's dress from yesterday.

Mr. MacIver was telling Master Jackie about the Negroes from Mount Vernon who'd been in Alexandria yesterday, and how his wife's servant girl had stolen a dress to sell at market and been whipped for it.

"Said she sold the dress to one of your Negroes," he finished. "My wife put great store in that dress. Come from England, through Philadelphia. And you know the boycott we've got on imported goods now."

"I'll question the servants." It was Mr. Lund's voice. "I promise you, the dress will be returned. We'll make good if it's been ruined. And whatever Negro stole it will be whipped."

Whipped! I trembled. Nobody around here could recollect anybody getting the lash. "Way back," Old Sinda had said to me, "way back, de gen'l had an' overseer, name of Crow, who took up de lash when it suited him. Gen'l never like it. He'd druther sell an incorrigible to de West Indies."

"My stepfather doesn't countenance whipping," Master Jackie said.

"Does he countenance one of our Negroes going to Alexandria and stealing?" Mr. Lund shot back. "I have to make an example of whoever did this."

I sat on the stairway, trembling. I heard the back door slam, heard Master Jackie mumble something about his stepfather not going to be happy. And knowing I would have his sympathy, I ran straightaway into the dining room.

"Master Jackie? Sir?"

He was at the table alone. A fire burned in the fireplace, everything on the table sparkled. He looked up.

"Oney, is something wrong with Miz Nelly or the baby?"

"No, sir, only please, I don't know who else to tell. If Lady Washington was here, she would listen."

He smiled. "Then you can tell me. What is it, child?"

68

"My mama has the dress. I heard Mr. MacIver in the hall. Oh, please, sir, don't let Mr. Lund whip my mama!"

He listened as I told how I'd been sent to barter brooms for it. "My mama's been wanting a pretty dress ever since I got my fine new clothes, sir. She didn't steal it."

"Ah, but Oney, you see, it was stolen property to begin with. Your mama should never have commerce with a Negro from another plantation. Most of what they bring to market is stolen."

"Please, Master Jackie, my mama didn't know it was stolen. Please don't let Mr. Lund whip her. Whip me instead."

"You?" He set down his linen napkin, pushed back his chair, and got up. "My mama would box my ears good if I let anything happen to you."

"Please don't let him whip my mama," I begged again.

He drew himself up to his full height. He was a good-looking man. Everybody said so. "I'll see what I can do, Oney. Have you had your breakfast yet?"

"No, sir."

"You were well spent when you got home yesterday morning. I'd like to punish your mama for dragging you to Alexandria. Well, go have Nathan give you breakfast, and don't worry. I'll not let Mr. Lund whip your mama. I'd have to answer to the general myself if I did. But I'm afraid she will have to be punished," he said.

"How?" I asked.

"Do as I say, Oney. And don't worry." And with that he took up his frock coat and went out of the house.

Mama was not whipped.

I was. By Mama.

Mr. Lund had the dress washed and ironed and returned that very day to Mrs. MacIver. And when I went to the servants' quarters to sleep that night, Mama was waiting for me.

In her hand was a switch. "You the one tol' Master Jackie I had the dress!" She came at me. I ran, but there was no running from Mama when she got this way. She leaped upon me like a fox on the chicken and beat me all over.

"You no-'count brat! 'Cause o' you I gots to be a hoe Negro now. I gots to work in the fields!"

Aunt Myrtilla rescued me, soothed me, stopped her. But Mama threw me out of the servants' quarters that night. Aunt Myrtilla brought me to the house. In the kitchen Nathan gave her some lard to put on my whip marks. In the dining room Master Jackie had guests for supper.

Frank and Austin, who waited on the table, came in to say we should hush all the noise. Master Jackie wanted to know what was going on.

They must have whispered it to Master Jackie when they brought in the whipped syllabub for dessert. Afterward he came into the kitchen to see for himself.

"Despicable," he said when he saw the swelling on my face and arms and legs. "I'm beginning to be sorry I didn't let Mr. Lund carry out his punishment."

I started to cry again. He hushed me, then called for Sall and told her that henceforth I was to sleep on the second floor of the kitchen building, with her and Caroline.

"My mama will not countenance anything happening to this child," he told her.

And so I was moved into the mansion house. From that day on, I never again slept in the servants' quarters. I slept in the house. I became a part of the family.

CHAPTER SEVEN
Summer 1777–Spring 1778

Mama in the fields. I tried not to think of it as I minded baby Eliza, as I bent over a cradle that seemed full of soft clouds on which she lay, gurgling happily.

Mama out in the hard summer sun. In the elegant quiet of the great white house I tried to pretend she was not out there, while Miz Nelly laughed softly with her friends over tea. Or Master Jackie entertained gentlemen in the west parlor.

I felt ashamed and guilty for Mama. Especially when Aunt Myrtilla came to the house now with a new seamstress she had been training, name of Esty. She was amiable and quiet.

I was doing some sewing now too. And many times when the summer was so wet, I looked out the window in our end of the kitchen and thought of Mama hoeing the corn.

And though she had treated me ill, I

missed her. She was my mother, the only one who really knew me. Yes, I liked sleeping on the second floor of the kitchen building with Sall and Caroline. I liked being dressed in fine feathers and eating food from the kitchen. It was better than the cornmeal and fish and sometimes meat the Negroes always ate.

The soft shadows, the sound of the pianoforte, the comforting glow of candles from silver holders, and the gentle voices and footfalls of the house comforted me.

I even liked hearing Mr. Lund arguing with Mr. Lanphier. I listened while Lanphier told him that currency was worthless and prices too high. He could not live with his wages.

"I'll throw in thirty barrels of corn if you stick to your work," Mr. Lund promised him.

Mr. Lanphier said it was not enough. He wanted the promise of some wool, too. Mr. Lund agreed. I listened, not believing how white people went about their business. And how they made that business getting paid for their work.

Lady Washington stayed home for Christmas. The general, she said, was in a place called Valley Forge. He wrote that his troops were hungry.

"And we're making nothing," I heard Mr. Lund grumble to Lady Washington. "All our wheat was destroyed this year from the weevil, our mills are idle, and we had a short crop of corn."

At the end of January, Lady Washington left to join her husband. A man name of Captain Triplett, from near Alexandria, came to attend her on the journey. We house servants loaded up the wagon that followed their carriage with as much food as we could.

"Roads are frozen." Mr. Lund turned to us house servants as we huddled in our cloaks, watching the caravan go down the road. "She will have a bad journey."

We muddled on. There was another shortage of salt. The spring was wet, and on Lady Washington's orders, all the house Negroes were inoculated for smallpox.

It was terrible. A doctor we did not know came to the house and scratched our arms with a small knife, and I was down sick for a week after. And when I awoke, Mr. Lund was gone to Valley Forge to bring home Mrs. Washington. It was May. Aunt Myrtilla told me that my mama would not take the inoculation because she was angry. She thought they were trying to kill her. She ran off for two days, and when she came back, the doctor was gone.

★ ★ ★

"Look how you've grown!" were Lady Washington's first words to me. "You are so tall! And pretty! And I hear you are becoming a first-rate seamstress."

I beamed under her praise. And our morning sewing sessions started again. Master Jackie and Miz Nelly moved to Abingdon, their new plantation near Alexandria. I no longer had to mind baby Eliza, and so once again I was free to accompany Lady Washington in all her duties.

She told me stories about the place called Valley Forge in the land of Pennsylvania.

"Most of the army was in tatters," she said as we quietly sat sewing. "Why, some of the men did not have hats, coats, shoes. They had no meat for days. Their muskets were covered with rust. Some would not come out of their log huts, for their nakedness. They had not been paid in months. Some just walked out of camp. Some stole from one another. Some went over to the enemy."

"What did the general do about soldiers that stole?" I asked.

"Oh, for stealing they were whipped soundly. Some with two hundred lashes."

I stopped sewing. My hands were cold in my lap. "The general whipped white people?"

"Oh yes, my dear. He had to keep order or he would lose his army. And the war."

Then she told me the names of others in the camp. "Mrs. Kitty Greene was there. She is the wife of Nathanael Greene, one of the general's most trusted officers. And oh, she is so pretty and gay. And Mrs. Lucy Knox, another officer's wife. And Lady Stirling. And the Marquis de Lafayette! Oh, you should meet him, and mayhap one day you will! He is a tall, young Frenchman come to give us aid. And he is only twenty years of age. Like my Jackie. But oh, he was lonely for his family. And many an hour he spoke of them to me."

I listened, as other children on the plantation listened to stories about Brer Fox and Brer Rabbit. "Baron Von Steuben. He is a Prussian officer who trains our men. He rises at three in the morning to smoke a pipe, drink coffee, and parade around before sunrise on his horse. He swears at the men in German. And when that does not take effect, he swears in French. And oh, then there is General Wayne. One day he took out a foraging party and brought back hundreds of beef cattle to save the men from starving."

In my bed at night I ran the pictures through my head. General Wayne looked like Nathan, bringing in the cows to be slaughtered and cooked. Baron Von Steuben appeared to me like Mr. Lund, cussing at Mr. Lanphier. And Kitty Greene like Miz Nelly, in silks, dancing.

And when the general had someone whipped, that someone was my mama.

1779

A year went by. Three wheat crops were ruined by weevils and bad weather. There was still another salt shortage. I made a whole apron for myself out of white cotton, and another for Sall and Caroline. By now Master Jackie and Miz Nelly had another little girl, name of Martha. Right before Christmas, Lady Washington was packing to leave again, this time for Philadelphia, where she would meet with the general, who would then take her on to the land of New Jersey again.

I learned more reading words. *Fruitcake. Raisins. Hickory nuts, shelled and chopped. Molasses pye.*

I had seen Mama only half a dozen times in the last year, never to speak to, always from a distance.

It was a Sunday evening when I was helping Lady Washington pack to go to Philadelphia. She sent me downstairs to fetch her a cup of coffee.

There I found Aunt Myrtilla and Mama in the kitchen.

I stood there like a jackass in the rain.

Aunt Myrtilla was putting lard on Mama's hands, which looked all sore and scraped.

Mama's dress was ragged. Her face dirty. But she was still so beautiful.

She said nothing. Her eyes gave no sign of knowing me. The door opened behind me then, and Nathan came into the kitchen, letting in a blast of cold air. I shivered. Nathan set a haunch of venison from the meat house down on the table.

"You ain't supposed to be in here, Betsy," he said.

"My fault," Aunt Myrtilla said. "I saw her hands in the servants' quarters this morning. I didn't think there would be harm in bringin' her in here to fix 'em."

"Negroes who are caught stealing are not allowed in the house," Nathan said. "Mr. Lund find out . . ." His voice trailed off.

"Hold on to your britches, Nathan," Aunt Myrtilla told him. "Ain't nobody stealin' anythin'."

"Somebody stole a bunch of the bricks piled outside for the piazza last night. Mr. Lund fit to be hog-tied."

She turned on him. "I didn't steal no bricks."

"Went to Alexandria market this mornin', didn't you? How'd you get those scraped hands?"

"Hoein'," Mama spit out at him.

"No corn to hoe in winter. Looks to me it's from haulin' bricks to Jack's wagon."

"Shut your face, Nathan," Aunt Myrtilla scolded.

"It's my kitchen," Nathan said.

"Kitchen belong to Hercules, if it belong to any Negro," Aunt Myrtilla snapped back.

They went on like that, and still I said nothing to my mama.

Mama, I wanted to say, *haven't I grown? Lady Washington said so. Don't you see it? Mama, I've missed you so. Don't you want to hold me? Mama?*

I must have said the word out loud. She looked at me.

"You say sumptin', little girl?" she asked.

"Mama, how are you keeping?"

She laughed. "There ain't no mama of your'n in this kitchen, little girl. You must be dreamin'."

I felt like I was a chicken in the jaws of a fox. Aunt Myrtilla gave her some bread and butter then, and a bowl of mush to take with her. She went out the kitchen door and never looked back.

A gust of cold air again and the slamming

of the door. "Doan pay no nevermind, honey, your mama like a porcupine in a trap these days," Aunt Myrtilla said.

Tears streamed down my face. Nathan set his work aside and knelt down on the stone floor. "Come on over here, little one," he said.

I went to him and he hugged me. "You gots your place right here," he whispered. "You hear me? You earned this place. Everybody like you. Your mama want to bring on her own ruination, nuthin' you can do. You gots me and Myrtilla and everybody. Right, Myrtilla?" He looked at her.

"Tha's right, chile. Best you break wif your mama anyways. All she talkin' 'bout these days is runnin' off. 'Spect she soon will," came the answer.

Another letter arrived from the general.

"You all best pay mind to your duties, now," Mr. Lund said when he gathered us to read it. "There's been too much slacking off, too many make-believe illnesses, and too much stealing. The general is thinking of selling some of you off."

There was dismay, shouts of "No, no," even some crying from the crowd gathered around him.

Mr. Lund read: " 'The advantages resulting from the sale of my Negroes I have very little doubt of. The only points, therefore, for me to consider, are first whether it would be most to my interest to have Negroes and the crops they will make or the sum they will now fetch. Though my scruples arise from a reluctance in offering these people at public vendue, if these poor wretches are to be held in a state of slavery, I do not see that a change of master will render it more irksome, provided husband, wife, and children are not separated from one another.' "

Mr. Lund stopped reading. "Y'all hear that? Now, y'all know the general won't sell anybody who won't agree to be sold. But I told him about Betsy over there" — he pointed to my mama in the back of the crowd — "and he said she should go up for sale if she don't stop stealing. It's up to you, Betsy. You gonna stop being a vexation to me? Or do I have to write the general and tell him?"

Mama agreed. She would stop being a vexation. No more stealing.

I had been standing in back of Mr. Lund, with the mansion Negroes. I felt so ashamed at Mama being fished out of the crowd that I turned and ran into the house.

"Is my mama stealing?" I asked Nathan later in the kitchen.

81

"That's what I hear, baby."

I worried for Mama. All I could think of was what Lady Washington had told me about soldiers at Valley Forge getting two hundred lashes for stealing. And though Mama wanted no more to do with me, I still worried for her.

CHAPTER EIGHT
Winter 1779-80

Another year went by. Lame Alice's daughter, Ariona, did die, and we buried her in the Negro cemetery. The general decided not to sell any Negroes, not even my mama.

Master Jackie and Miz Nelly had a third daughter. And this one, also named Nelly, came to live at Mount Vernon, brought there by Lady Washington.

Miz Nelly was too ill to care for her. We had another baby in the house, and I was once more brought to the nursery at times to mind her.

Lady Washington told me about the terrible winter at Morristown in the land of New Jersey, when the general's men coughed and died and starved again.

"Give me a list of the number and kinds of horses I possess," the general wrote. "With the ages, colors, and sexes. Have you made good the decayed trees at the ends of the house? Have you made any attempts to reclaim more land for the meadow? An account of these things would be satisfactory to me and infinitely amusing in the recital, as I have these improvements very much at heart."

"He is homesick," Lady Washington told me. "But perhaps the war will be over soon. The French have come to our aid."

Mr. Lund took himself a wife, his cousin, name of Elizabeth. He brought her to the mansion house to live. She was a thin, anxious lady. When Lady Washington was off visiting the general that winter, Elizabeth was in charge of the household.

She was very religious. Twice a day she made all the house servants kneel and pray, and she told us how we would burn in hell for our sins.

"What sins do I have?" I asked Nathan.

"Oney," he said. "White people got lists of sins we don't even know about. They gots plenty of reason to stay on their knees for hours."

I wondered what those sins could be.

Spring 1780

It was spring. You could smell the river. The strawberry vines and fruit trees were already giving their bounty. I was near eight and coming on to being sassy. Lady Washington was away, visiting the general in the land of New York. Yesterday old Father Jack, Sam, and Schomberg had the general's schooner out and brought in a good load of shad. Mr. Lund was pleased. "I can get two hundred pounds cash for it in Alexandria's market sheds," he said. "And the plantation needs the money."

Then he told us that Charleston, South Carolina, had fallen to the British.

I had just come out of the house after putting baby Nelly down for her nap. I stood on the front grass and smelled the spring, the newly budding trees, the honeysuckle vines, the dogwood and redbud.

Everything was so peaceful. But then from the direction of the kitchen came the sound of Hercules yelling. "I tol' you I makin' roe fer supper! Not duck!" Then there came a crashing of a pot. Or likely one of Lady Washington's copper kettles.

For a moment it drowned out the sound of the bell down at the stables. And then Sambo Anderson's voice.

"Sloops in the river! Sloops in the river!"

Negroes came running. From the clover fields, the cornfields, the stables, the washhouse, the meat house.

We'd been expecting this. Mr. Lund had spoken of British raids near Dumfries, in which Negroes had been stolen.

I ran across the grass toward the river, where the other Negroes were gathering. And I saw the king's ship on the Maryland shore, saw some men lower a small boat and a man in a blue coat get into it along with some red-coated men.

Then they started rowing to the general's wharf.

Mr. Lund had come to stand at the edge of the lawn. In his hand he had a musket. Sambo Anderson stood there with his old musket too. "Giles," Mr. Lund said without turning, "are the horses hid?"

"Yessir."

"You Negroes, get back to the quarters," he ordered. They backed off but stayed. More than a dozen of them had come from the house and the fields. I saw my mama edging her way forward, Aunt Myrtilla standing next to her, her hand on Mama's arm.

The small boat made its way to the general's wharf, and three men jumped out and came up the path to where we were standing.

Mr. Lund held on to his musket. The man who stood in front of him in the blue coat was long in the face and pale, with eyes that darted this way and that, like a rabbit chased by a hound. He wore lots of lace at his wrists. His breeches were silk.

"Is this the home of Mr. Washington?" he asked.

"It is the home of General Washington," Mr. Lund said.

"Quite. Is Mr. Washington at home, then?"

"No. The general is not heah."

"Is his lady?"

"Lady Washington isn't heah, either."

The sallow face smiled, showing uneven teeth as the eyes lighted on Mrs. Lund, who had come to stand next to her husband. "Is this not Lady Washington?" And the man bowed.

"This is my wife, sir."

" 'Straordinary," he said.

"She and I are stewards of this place while the general and his lady are away at war," Mr. Lund told him.

"At losing a war," the man corrected.

"That has yet to be determined," Mr. Lund answered.

"Quite." Now the man looked around, taking in everything — the white house sitting on the hill, the stables, the fields, the trees and walks and flowers, the outbuildings. "An elegant seat," he said.

In his blue coat with the shiny buttons and gold lace, his high-polished boots and snow white breeches, the sword at his side, he was like something you dreamed if you ate too many sweetmeats.

"Your Mr. Washington has a lovely place here. We are in need of supplies. Victuals. What can you provision us with?"

"Our meadows have been injured by uncommon rain this spring," Mr. Lund said. "Last yeah the wheat had an infestation of the weevil. Because trade with the West Indies has stopped, the mill stands idle most of the time. We lack salt to put up herring."

"Livestock?"

"They're doing poorly."

"Nevertheless, Mr. . . . what did you say your name was?"

"Mr. Washington. Lund Washington."

"Ah, a relative?"

"A cousin."

"Well!" He bowed again. "I am Captain Richard Graves of the HMS *Savage*, sloop of war. I insist you provision us. My marines are well armed, and I can see you have no defenses. It would distress me to have to burn the house and fields of so noble a man as your Mr. Washington."

"General Washington," Mr. Lund said again.

"A fire would scarce make the distinction, now, would it, Mr. Lund Washington?"

We all knew what Mr. Lund was supposed to say. What he'd promised the general he'd say. And do, in the event of an attack. Nathan had told me. "He 'posed to drive off any British landing party with muskets. He 'posed to let them burn the place but never give 'em a thing," Nathan had said.

Captain Graves turned and pointed across the river. "You see that, Mr. Lund Washington?" he asked.

We looked.

On the Maryland side we saw flames and smoke rising above the trees. Some of the smoke was black and it drifted with the breeze across the mile-wide river, so we could smell it.

Mr. Lund spoke: "When the general engaged in the contest, he put all to stake, suh. He is well aware of the exposed situation of his house and property. He has given me orders, by no means, to comply with any demands. He is ready to meet the fate of his neighbors."

"Fool! You Americans are all fools." Then he turned and gave orders to one of his men to move the sloop to the Virginia side of the river. "Once more I ask, Mr. Lund Washington. We need provisions. A few hens, slabs of bacon, a leg of mutton, some sugar, coffee, and victuals to dress up our table. A small matter, surely, to save Mr. Washington's home."

I saw Mr. Lund's shoulders sag, saw the musket set, butt end on the ground. "Sall," he ordered quietly, "Nathan, see what you can fetch from the meat house. Caroline, get that brace of ducks that Hercules was screamin' about. Along with some coffee and sugar." He reached into a pocket, took out the keys to the meat house, and gave them to Nathan.

He was not about to drive off anybody. He spoke softly with Captain Graves, away from the rest of us so we could not hear. Then he turned to his wife.

"I'm going aboard the sloop for a while," he said. "See that the victuals are brought aboard."

Captain Graves bowed to Mrs. Lund, and they turned to go. Then Captain Graves hesitated.

"We could use some Negroes," he said.

Mr. Lund seemed taken aback. "You said victuals."

"I have the authority from His Royal Majesty to grant liberty to the Negroes if they will serve us."

Mr. Lund said nothing. He knew about such authority. I'd heard him speaking of it.

Captain Graves stepped forward, walking

a little more up the hill on the tender spring grass. He addressed the Negroes who were standing a bit off, watching.

"Freedom!" His voice rang out. "Liberty for any and all of you who deign to join the king's forces! What say you?"

There was silence at first, then mumblings among them.

I saw Nathan and Sall coming from the meat house. Nathan had a haunch of meat on one shoulder. Sall carried some chickens. At the same time, Caroline came out of the mansion house with the ducks and a basket of victuals.

"What say you to taking the liberty your master says he is fighting for? Think you that when he returns, if he returns, he will let you share in its blessing?"

More mumblings from the crowd.

"Come now." Captain Graves clasped his hands behind his back and addressed them like children. "Serve us, who have given liberty so freely to all of your race who have joined us."

I held my breath. Movement started, like an underground current in a spring stream. I saw Frederick step forward, then Frank, then Gunner. They shuffled at first. Captain Graves smiled and held out his hand and encouraged them.

"Don't leave," Mr. Lund begged each one as they passed him. "It's your choice. Y'all don't hafta go."

Old Peter, Lewis, Harry, Tom, Stephen, James, Watty, Daniel, Lucy, Esther, Deborah, and then, oh no!

My mama! Aunt Myrtilla tried to stay her, hand on Mama's arm. "What's the matter wif you, Betsy! You gots a chile here!"

Captain Graves pulled Aunt Myrtilla away. "Cease this nonsense in the name of His Majesty! If you are too dim-witted to take freedom, she is not!"

He pushed Aunt Myrtilla, who stumbled toward me.

"Mama!" I cried.

He turned to me, his eyes going over my person. "You're a likely wench. What say you? Want to come along?"

Aunt Myrtilla put a protecting arm around my shoulder. "She Lady Washington's special girl," she told him.

"Is she, now?" He stepped toward me, put a hand under my chin, and raised it so I had to look at him. "Quite a comely lass. I could use her to wait my table."

Sambo Anderson stepped forward then, holding his old musket up. "You leave her be! She jus' a chile!"

Now the attention of the captain was on

Sambo. "A Negro with a musket. Mr. Washington must indeed be lenient."

"He hunts," Nathan said. He stood there with the haunch of meat on his shoulder, tall and proud.

"He hunts, does he?" Captain Graves asked. "And what do you do?"

"I cook."

"I could use a cook."

"He hunts at night," Nathan said quietly. "In the dark. He's a good shot in the dark. In daylight he's even better."

Everyone stood stock-still for a moment. The captain's eyes went from one of us to the other. He saw Mrs. Lund exchange looks with the remaining Negroes, who seemed to have moved closer of a sudden. He saw Sambo with the musket, Nathan with the haunch of meat on his shoulder, standing taller than him. He knew he stood alone, that his men were gone down to the wharf.

And then he saw Caroline, who had the basket of victuals in her hand, covered with a linen napkin, which she raised now.

Under it was a gleaming knife.

Captain Graves took out his lacy handkerchief and waved it at us. "Bring the victuals aboard."

"We bring them to the small boats," Nathan said.

Captain Graves looked around again. "Quite," he said. And Nathan and Caroline and Sall followed him down the path to the wharf.

And I stood there watching them until the victuals were loaded and they pushed off. They took one of the general's keelboats, a long one, to put the Negroes in.

I held my breath until Caroline, Sall, and Nathan came back up the path. I might never see Mama again. Nathan had to take me in hand and bring me into the mansion house.

My mama was one of the Gone.

CHAPTER NINE
Spring 1780–Fall 1781

Mr. Lund put words about my mama in the *Virginia Gazette*. Nathan showed me the words.

RUNAWAY

On Friday last, a young high yellow Negro wench named Betsy, sought by Mr. Lund Washington of Mount Vernon Plantation. She is well known in this part of the county. A good mistress of the needle. Twenty pounds sterling for her head or five pounds to any person that secures her in the workhouse. To be paid by Lund Washington.

Mama was a runaway, the worst thing you could be on the plantation.

Mr. Lund's spirit got so cast down in the months after his Negro servants left that we learned to stay away from him.

But I could not stay away from his wife. She was everywhere in the house, running things. She poked her nose in the kitchen and into the pots. One day before Christmas, she told Hercules he was using too much sugar in a cake.

"Sugar is so dear," she complained. "I scarce have enough for my coffee. Couldn't we sacrifice cake, so we can have sugar on the table?"

Nobody told Hercules what to do in the kitchen. He picked up the cone of sugar and chopped it up. Then he put it in a bowl, walked across the kitchen, and threw it into the fire in the hearth.

"Sugar sacrificed," he said. "No more cake. Now get outta my kitchen."

Mrs. Lund backed out, her mouth open. "My husband will hear of this," she warned.

"Good. Then you do the cookin'. I quits."

"No, no," Mrs. Lund begged. "Please don't, please. I'll stay out of the kitchen."

She never came into the kitchen again after that, and it was where I went to get free of her.

Because sugar continued to be so dear, Mr. Lund became mad with the idea of pressing cornstalks to get molasses. He had the servants doing this for days. I thought that if we soon did not have an end to the war, we would soon have an end to Mr. Lund.

Then word went around that he had been scolded in a letter by the general for not letting the British burn the place.

Nathan saw the letter lying on a desk in the west parlor and told us of it.

"General in a temper 'cause Mr. Lund boarded their sloop," Nathan whispered to me and Hercules in the kitchen. " 'Cause Mr. Lund provision them. 'Cause he not fire on them."

When Mr. and Mrs. Lund were out visiting, Nathan brought me into the west parlor and showed me the general's writing.

" 'It would have been less painful to me,' " Nathan read, " 'if they burned my house. Less painful if they laid my plantation in ruins. To go on board their vessel, to carry them refreshments, to commune with a parcel of plundering scoundrels, to ask the surrender of my Negroes, was ill judged.' "

We had not known until then that Mr. Lund had asked the captain for the return of my mama and the others.

No small reason Mr. Lund's spirits were down.

No small reason his wife's were too. She and her prayerful ways wore me down. She made me kneel every day on the hard floor in her room and pray for the soul of my mama. One day she decided I should kneel alone and pray.

She made me kneel for two hours.

"The good Lord alone knows the whereabouts of your mama," she said. "He alone knows to what depravity she is exposed. Pray that she will resist all immoral practices. Pray that she remembers her first loyalty, her duty to God and then to her master, that the Lord will deliver her home, out of the land of Egypt."

I didn't know my mama was in Egypt. I did know that she would remember her first loyalty, though. And that it was to herself.

Every day, between chores, Mrs. Lund made me kneel for at least an hour and pray for Mama. There was no escape. I was about to escape to Dogue Run Farm and get Old Sinda to give me a conjure bag to put under her bed and make her nice, when one day Mr. Lund said he needed me.

He had found a market in Boston for some flour. The plantation needed money. But the flour he had in storage had soured, and he wanted it tossed to get rid of the dampness.

"Enough praying," he told his wife. "I need the girl to toss some flour."

So I was sent to the storehouse. It was July and very hot. In the storehouse the children soon made a game of the job, throwing the flour up into the air to rid it of dampness.

I was full of flour when I was summoned to the house by Caroline. My hair was white, my face smudged with it, and I dragged it into the house on my feet and brushed it off my clothing when I stood before Lady Washington.

She was home. The house was in a flurry. "The war is moving south," she said. "I pray it will soon be over. Oh, Oney, what have you been about?"

"Tossing flour, ma'am. In the storehouse, for Mr. Lund."

"I told them you weren't to work outside the house, didn't I? Oney child, come here. I am so weary from my journey. Fetch me some lemonade and see what sweets are in the kitchen. A piece of cake, perhaps. I have been longing for some of Hercules' cake."

"No cake, ma'am," I said. "Hercules won't make any cake. He had a fight with Mrs. Lund."

She was unhooking her English gown. "Come help me with this, Oney, there's a good child. Well, I'm home now, and I say there will be cake. Tell Hercules I require my great cake for supper. And from henceforth you are going to be my personal maid. I have given it much thought on the way home. And the general agrees. What say you?"

"I would most admire to be your personal maid," I said, "but what about Sally?"

"She is old now and becoming blind. She will teach you. I'm sad to hear that your mother was taken away, Oney. Has anyone heard where she is?"

"In Egypt, ma'am."

She stared at me. She blinked. "In Egypt?"

"Yes, that's what Mrs. Lund says. I have to kneel on the floor every day and pray that she gets returned to us from Egypt."

She slipped out of her English gown. I took it from her and handed her the tabby silk sacque she lounged about in and the cap trimmed with lace that she favored. "There will be no more kneeling and praying for your mama, Oney," she said. "I'm hoping the general will be able to come home soon for a visit. There is much to do."

Word came to us in September of '81. The general was in a place called Head of Elk in the land of Maryland. He should reach Williamsburg on the fifteenth.

Never was the house in such confusion.

He had not been home in six years.

Master Jackie and his Nelly came with three more of their children, one a new baby, name of George Washington Parke Custis. Just a mite he was, not as long as his name.

The house was made ready, inside and out. Floors and windows shone. All the china and silver and glassware were fetched home from a neighbor's barn. Everything was dusted, polished, fluffed, brushed, and swept. In the flower garden there were still blooms, and hummingbirds whirring about them.

Chickens, ducks, pigs, were slaughtered. Ice was gotten up from the dry well in the cellar. Pies and cakes were made. The horses were groomed, chairs were lined up straight in the large parlor, the boxwood trimmed, the bowling green and curving drives neatened.

As Lady Washington's personal maid, I never left her side. I visited the meat house with her, the weavers' cottage, the buttery, the poultry yard, the kitchen garden. I counted blankets for her, made sure all eight bedchambers on the second and third floors had a goodly supply of candles, bed warmers, and towels, perfumed powder for the hair. I sat next to her while she planned meals.

She took me with her to Alexandria. I rode with her in the carriage, dressed in my best, holding her basket. She knew a merchant there who could supply her with a case of pickles, salad oil, even India mangoes, and a large Cheshire cheese, eight pounds of coffee, almonds in the shell, and raisins. Nathan went with us to help fetch it all home.

As we walked along the street she told me how her husband, when just a young man, had been a surveyor. "He laid out the first town plan for this place," she said. "He always had a surveyor's eye."

And then finally, one day in late September, the general came riding up the lane through the west gate.

Many men were with him on horses that pranced. Men in bright uniforms, men wearing swords, men who had been to war, with tall dusty boots, colorful sashes, loud voices — hungry men. Some spoke in a strange tongue. French, Nathan said.

And, on his own horse, name of Chinkling, came home Billy Lee, the Negro who had been at the general's side through all of the war so far.

Sally had taught me to dress Lady Washington's hair, lay out her gowns. Old Sally was feeble now, near seventy, and as she oversaw me the first night the general was home, as I ran about the bedroom fetching things, she said, "Lord, chile, you are sprightly. And bright. Yes, you will do fine. You will."

From belowstairs came the laughter of men, the clinking of glasses. Miz Nelly was playing the pianoforte. Frank and Austin, the household waiters, were dressed in new livery. Sall and Caroline were wearing crisp, colorful cotton, the whitest of aprons and caps, and neckerchiefs. So was I. My new dress was blue, like the summer sky, and had an underskirt the color of cinnamon.

I had seen the general when I was a child, but I did not remember him. From Lady Washington I knew he was near six feet three, strong, and that his face was marked from the pox.

I had studied his portrait that hung in the west parlor. It did not show signs of the pox on his face. He was very handsome.

I stared at the portrait a long time, trying to figure out which was the surveyor's eye.

CHAPTER TEN

Old Sally had schooled me in many important things about being Lady Washington's personal maid. But one thing she said with great care.

"Betimes she likes to talk. When she do, you listen."

That first night the general was home, Lady Washington talked while I dressed her hair.

"The general scarce speaks to his own mama," she said. "She lives in Fredericksburg. Did you ever hear the story of what happened to her while she was carrying the general in her womb?"

"No, ma'am."

"She was at dinner with her family. Lightning struck the house and hit a young girl at table with them. The poor thing died on the spot. And it gave a jolt to the general's mother. She is terrible afraid of lightning. And of many other things."

I must tell Old Sinda about that, I decided. She would likely say what happened to the general's mother was the power of conjure.

I did not meet the general until the following day. Most of the men who had come with him, the counts and generals in white breeches, were out of the house, riding. Master Jackie was showing them about the place.

Lady Washington took me by the hand and brought me to his study at the south end of the house. "Few people are allowed in here," she whispered.

It was a plain room, no rugs on the floor, no drapes at the windows. September sunshine shone in. "General Washington!" Lady Washington stood there in the doorway, holding my hand. "I would like to present to you my new personal maid and companion, Oney Judge."

He was seated at his desk. He stood up. Yes, he was tall, very tall. And straight, like a tree, like the joints that held up his house.

I curtsied, as she had taught me. "Your servant, sir," I said.

He stepped out from behind his desk. "Well, and so this is the Oney Judge I've heard so much about. As I recollect, your father was Andrew Judge, a very competent carpenter."

"Yessir."

I looked at him. *The eyes,* I thought, *never have I seen such eyes.* There was a sternness in them that made you cringe. God would have eyes like that. And yet even while I thought, *He knows all my sins. And my daddy's and mama's sins, too,* there was at the same time a light in those eyes, a kindness that fell on me like the September sun.

"I have cause to be away from my wife much in this war, Oney," he said. "It eases my mind to know that someone as bright and young and loyal as you will be at her side. Carry out your duties well, child."

His voice was soft, but the words were a command. This man expected much from people he allowed near him. After all, his mama had been struck by lightning when she carried him.

That had been God doing a good fix on him. All you had to do was see the way he bore himself to know it.

I curtsied again and turned to leave. He was very busy. Lady Washington had said that the Frenchman, Lafayette, had British general Cornwallis penned up at Yorktown. That in the Chesapeake another Frenchman, name of the Comte de Grasse, had twenty-eight ships of war and three thousand more Frenchmen waiting to fight.

The general expected much from them.

"Oney," The voice stopped me. "I heard that your mama ran off with the British."

"Yessir," I mumbled.

"Well, I am trying to find her. And the others. I fear the British will misuse them. Perhaps when the war is over, we shall find her, child."

I could think of nothing to say. I stood there like the wagon horse, head bowed. Then, when Mrs. Washington nudged me I ran from the room.

I was taken with the general. But he stayed for only five days. In those five days Lady Washington spread herself all over the place, and it seemed as if we did nothing but run from the meat house and the larder to the kitchen, to her private bedroom, to the dining room. "After all," she told me, "we are entertaining the general, the Comte de Rochambeau, and his staff."

And then Master Jackie and Miz Nelly's four children were all over the place. And Miz Nelly, seeing how I attended Lady Washington, asked to borrow me once or twice to dress her hair.

I fell into bed well spent at night.

Then, in the middle of all the bustle, the elegant dinners, there came a trouble. It went through the house like the smoke from the men's pipes. It sat in the air.

Master Jackie wanted to go to war.

Master Jackie wanted to go with his step-papa to Yorktown.

I heard the words between Master Jackie and Miz Nelly. I was in their bedchamber, dressing her hair.

They spoke as if I were not there. Sally had told me to expect this, too. "White peoples will sometimes say things to each other in front of you. Give no never mind to you bein' in the room. Like you a chair. If they do, you act like a chair."

"How do I act like a chair?"

"Do a chair talk? Do a chair allow that it hear sumpthin'? Do a chair tell what it hear?"

So I acted like a chair.

"Four children!" Miz Nelly said. "You have four children. Have you no thought for them?"

"I've promised Papa to stay out of the way of the musket fire," Master Jackie said. He lounged in a chair, his long legs stretched out. "This is going to be the last battle of the war, Nelly. I can't miss it."

"Your steppapa has kept you out of the war at your mama's request. Now you expect him to make you a colonel?"

"I am to be his volunteer aide-de-camp," Master Jackie told her. "I don't expect to be made a colonel."

"If anything happens to you, I'll never forgive you, Jackie." Miz Nelly held a lace handkerchief to her mouth.

"What could happen?" Master Jackie yawned. "Except lots of joviality. Victory dinners and meeting all the enemy officers at the end. I can't miss out on it, Nelly. I just can't."

But I wanted to talk to Billy Lee, the man who had been all through the war with the general. I'd seen him rushing about in the mansion house the last few days, always attending the general. I'd seen how everybody gave way to him.

One afternoon I found him outside when he was polishing the general's boots.

"What you wanta know 'bout?" he asked me. "Trenton? Most of the chillens wanta know 'bout Trenton. Or Monmouth. They been crawlin' all over me since I come home, like fire ants."

"Tell me why the general doesn't talk to his mama," I said.

Billy Lee scowled at me. "What you wanta know that for?"

" 'Cause me and my mama fight all the time."

He nodded. "I heard she run off."

"Yes."

"All right. But what I say, you keep to yourself. Kin you do that?"

"I attend Lady Washington," I told him. "Like you attend the general. I can act like a chair. Sally taught me."

He laughed at that. "Good ole Sally. You learn from her, you learn a lot. Well, for one thing, the general's mama be a Tory. She on the side of the king. An' she never forgive him for fightin' the king's people. You know what they do to Tories hereabouts. All the other Tories in Fredericksburg been tarred an' feathered. Burned out. Onliest thing protect her is that she the general's mama."

"What else?" I asked.

He snorted. "That lady so tight, she never give the general a shilling for his schoolin' when he young. He was supposed to go to England to school, like his halfbrother, Lawrence. But then his daddy die, an' his mama hold on to the money like a fox hold on to a chicken. He want music lessons, she loan him the money. He gotta pay it back."

I nodded, waiting.

"When he young, he wanta go to sea. She won't let him go. If it weren't for Lawrence, who take him under his wing when he be a little boy, I doan know how he grow up. You think she be proud of him now? She don't give a hen's tooth if he be commander in chief. I seed overseers with a whip in hand more lovin' than that lady. An' then she goes to the gov'm'nt in Virginny an' says she needs money. Asks for a pension. Jus' to embarrass him."

"Why did she do all this?" I asked.

"Jus' natural mean, she is. But the general, now, he got the mettle to go up against her. An' I been with him when his glass be runnin' low. An' sometimes I think if he didn't have the mettle to fight the old lady, he never have it to go up against the British."

Billy Lee shook his head. "He command a whole army, but he never do know how to talk wif her. Everythin' he do, she say is wrong."

"Everything I did, my mama said was wrong," I told him.

"I guess it doan matter if you be Negro or white, you still need a mama's love," Billy Lee said.

"Is it true you've been with the general for years, Billy?"

He chuckled. "He buy me in '68. I called Mulatto Will then. I jus' a little older than you. I go for sixty-one pounds an' fifteen shillings."

"And you hunted with him before the war."

"I the only one he ever want to hunt wif him. Now, you wanta hear 'bout Trenton?"

I said yes. And so he told me about Trenton. And Monmouth. And Long Island. And Valley Forge.

CHAPTER ELEVEN

The houseguests were still sleeping. The house was quiet.

In the upstairs hall I overheard Billy Lee's voice. "After this be over, sir, I sure would like to bring my wife here from Philadelphia. She is called Margaret Thomas."

"I want to accommodate you, Billy," came the general's answer. "You have lived with me long and followed my fortunes through the war with fidelity. But a free Negro on this place? How will my people feel?"

The general spoke of us as "his people."

"I know, sir. I been studyin' on that proper. She could live in Alexandria, an' I could visit."

"We'll see, Billy, we'll see."

I did not know that Billy had taken him a wife.

And then I heard something else.

"I dearly wish I could recover my people who ran off with the British," the general said. "I've heard accounts that the British are treating all Negroes who went with them ill. That they are being made to dig trenches near Williamsburg. That they use the women to scrub their clothing, that anyone who refuses to wait on the officers is sent to the West Indies."

"Bad business, General," I heard Billy answer. "But maybe we kin get 'em back when we go to Yorktown."

I was so frightened for Mama. I knew she would sass any British officers she was made to serve.

I hurried to Lady Washington's chamber to deliver the petticoat I was supposed to bring. *Oh, Mama,* I thought, *why did you ever run?*

When the general, Billy Lee, and the other soldiers left later that day, in a flurry of packing and promises, toasts and good wishes, Master Jackie went with them.

The house settled down again, and every morning I was invited into Lady Washington's bedchamber with the other favored seamstresses to sew and chat. And I had a position of eminence. The others knew it. I was her favorite. They cast sly, envious looks at me.

In the weeks that followed, I helped sew a

silk ball gown the color of salmon. And now it was Lady Washington who read us the general's letters.

" 'I have been honored by touching the first spark to the French cannon,' " she read. " 'Our siege guns are placed only a few hundred yards from the enemy's lines. De Grasse has agreed to stay, with his armada, until the end of October. I do not know what may be in the womb of fate, but we are well supplied with troops, artillery, and provender.' "

And, " 'Never have I lived so comfortably in the course of an engagement. Our household lists sixty-two turkeys, thirty-nine ducks, one hundred two chickens, just to name some of it. And a variety of fruit and vegetables.' "

Another read: " 'Some of my people are here, ill used by the British. Frederick and Frank have sought me out and given intelligence about some others. They are in hiding in the woods, sick with the pox. It has been said the British had them infected in hopes of their carrying the smallpox to the Americans.' "

Lady Washington looked up from the letter, across the room, at me. "He does not say which ones, Oney," she said. "Let us pray one is not your mama."

Then, finally, the letter Lady Washington had been awaiting. " 'This day, the nineteenth, the British lay down their arms.' "

Then another letter, delivered by a horseman who came pounding on the door late at night, so that Mr. Lund picked up his musket before he answered. And white and Negro folk alike trembled.

"Who is it? What brings you at this hour?" Mr. Lund, lantern in hand, called out before he opened the door.

"I've a message for Mrs. Washington. Make haste and open," came the muffled cry.

The door was opened. The man came in. Mr. Lund held out his hand, and the letter was handed over. Lady Washington, in her sacque and lace night bonnet, came into the hall. "What is it, Lund? Is it bad news?"

Candles were lit. Lady Washington read, then clasped the paper to her bosom. "Oh, my Jackie is grevious ill. He has camp fever! The general has sent him to Eltham, his aunt's house. Oh, I must go. Nelly! Nelly dear!" They hugged each other.

"I must have my things packed. And Nelly's. We will leave now!" Lady Washington said.

"Nighttime is no time to be about on the roads, ma'am," Mr. Lund said. "Not in these times."

116

"I go to Eltham now!" Lady Washington insisted. Then her eyes found me. "Oney, pack my things. Caroline, pack Miz Nelly's. Don't wake the children. Oney, pack your things too. You shall accompany me."

Secretly my spirit was high. Lord forgive me. This middle-of-the-night leave-taking had about it an air of things to happen. I had been off the plantation before, yes, but only as far as Alexandria.

Mr. Lund and Paris accompanied us on horseback. Giles, from the stables drove. On the way we stopped on the dark road at an appointed spot. There was an elderly Negro man on horseback. Next to him, sitting on a small trunk, was a likely Negro girl a little older than me. She was Miz Nelly's personal maid. Her name was Violet.

"Good, Old Peter and Violet are here," Miz Nelly said.

The girl got into the carriage. The man rode with Mr. Lund. In the night the carriage rocked. Miz Nelly cried and sniffed until she fell asleep. Soon Lady Washington dozed too. Violet leaned across and whispered to me.

"Miz Nelly sent word I should pack her mourning dress. Did you pack Lady Washington's?"

"I packed a black dress," I said, "but I didn't think it was for mourning."

"What did you think it was for, silly?" she chided me. Then she kicked me. "Heard your mama run off."

"Yes."

"Old Peter out there, he jus' come back from where she be. He say the king's men use up the women who come with them. You know what that means. Don't you?"

I shook my head no, though I did. I turned to look out the carriage window. Outside flared the torches of Mr. Lund, Paris, and Old Peter. Soon I fell asleep too and did not even waken when we crossed the Pamunkey River on the ferry.

Our first day at Eltham, Lady Washington and Miz Nelly spent the whole time in Master Jackie's bedchamber with Dr. Craik, who had ridden over from Yorktown.

Violet and I spent our free time in the kitchen. There were half a dozen Negroes in the house of Lady Washington's brother-in-law. And they all knew about the slaves who'd run off and were at Yorktown.

But Old Peter knew the most. I sat and listened while he told of it. "Dey been worn down diggin' trenches for de king's men. Den, when de shootin' start, dey turned

118

adrift. No wages. Some of dem got de smallpox. An' dey be sent to de 'Merican lines but get turned away. So dey hightail it to de woods. I been to de woods. I see dem hidin' dere, a whole bunch of 'em, afeared to come out. Afeared of de gunfire. We heard de music on de day de king's men surrender. 'Yankee Doodle.' "

"I'm afraid my mother is there," I said.

"You best hope she not be," Old Peter advised. "Dese people afeared to go to de 'Mericans, afeared to go back to de British. Some gonna die dere in de woods."

Jane, the head cook, was kneading dough. She was brisk. "If any of those slaves in the woods are General Washington's, he'll get them back," she said.

Old Peter nodded.

That evening the general himself arrived, with Billy Lee. He went right upstairs, but Billy came into the kitchen.

"Hard ride," he said. "General want to make it in one day. What's the word on Master Jackie?"

"They say he not gonna live," Jane told him.

Billy Lee was given food. I watched him eat. "Did the general find any of his runaways?" I asked.

Billy Lee swallowed, wiped his mouth,

119

and looked at me. "Yes," he said. "He found three. Your mama one of 'em. He sendin' 'em home under guard."

I felt a rush of joy. "Mama is alive, then?"

"She had the pox," Billy said. "Her pretty face ain't so pretty anymore. But she's comin' home."

Master Jackie died that night. We stayed five days at Eltham. Violet had her hands full with Miz Nelly, who was near to collapsing. Lady Washington was saddened but brave.

The silk dress the color of salmon was put aside. The first-mourning dress was brought out. When we got home to Mount Vernon, there was black crepe draped over the front doorway.

I attended Lady Washington and stayed close to her. The general was home but planned to go to Philadelphia at the end of the month. Lady Washington was to go with him.

After two days at home I finally found a chance to slip out of the house and find my mama.

My mama had been home for near a week and hadn't come out of her cabin. As I approached, Old Sinda came walking toward me.

"Your mama's face all ruint. But her mind worse. I mix up herbs, asafetida, gunpowder, sulfur, salt, red candle wax, goofer dust. Got dat midnight last from Master Jackie's grave." She chuckled. "It's always good to get goofer dust from a new grave from a good Christian like Master Jackie. Gather it afore midnight if de root is fer good, just after if it be fer evil workins'. I wuz careful not to give offense to de spirits. Anyways, Master Jackie's spirit not dere. It out makin' its rounds at midnight. I left a shillin' fer payment, so he doan follow me home."

"What will your root do for my mama?"

"Bring her head to rights. Bring down de mens what ruint her."

I moved toward the cabin door. She put a hand on my arm. "Jus' one thing. Lady Washington know what's good fer dose granchillens of hers, she let dem pass over Master Jackie's grave. Master Jackie love dose chillens. If dey doan pass back and forth over de grave, he gonna come and visit 'em. Likely dey get fretful and won't sleep. You tell her dat."

"I will," I said. Though I knew I would not. I dared not even let Lady Washington know I was here this day.

CHAPTER TWELVE

She was lying on a pallet in the corner of the cabin. The only other furniture was a wooden table and one chair. She lay under a dirty quilt. The hearth smoked.

"Mama?" I walked softly to the bed.

"Umm?"

"Mama, how are you keeping?"

"Who is it?"

"It's me. Oney."

She blinked, and her brown eyes went over me like she'd never seen me before. She never raised her head.

"Oney? My little girl?"

I felt a rush of love. I knelt down by the bed. "Yes, Mama. Are you still sickly?"

She sat up, looked around as if she didn't know where she was, and wiped her eyes. "Lordy, did I sleep. What day is this?"

"Monday."

"What month?"

"November, Mama. They brought you

home. You're home from Yorktown. They said you had the pox."

She remembered then. Her hands went over her face. Then she covered her face with those hands and wept silently. "I never gonna be pretty no more. And my looks is all I had."

"Oh, Mama, you're still you." I reached out to her.

She pushed me away angrily. "My looks is all I *had!* You think I doan know that? I wuz goin' places. That British officer said he'd take me back to England wif him! Said I'd be treated like a lady there! Then afore I know what's goin' on, he sends me to care for another Negro servant who had the pox. And when I come down wif it, sick as a dog, he sends me on a mission!" She laughed. "A mission! Wif a letter to the 'Mericans. Said I should get close as I could to them. Infect them, an' he'd take care of me! And when I come back, he push me outta his tent! Said if I come back, he'd shoot me. I hadda go to the woods an' live!"

"But you're home now, Mama."

"Home? Home?" She pushed the quilt aside and stood up. "You call *this* home?"

Then she saw me again. In another way. "Look at those fancy clothes you're wearin'."

"Mama, I have to dress like this. All house

servants do. I'm Lady Washington's personal girl now. I just got back from Eltham with her. Master Jackie died."

Her eyes went wide. "Master Jackie?"

"He had camp fever."

"He wuz good to me. An' you."

"I know. But that's why I'm dressed like this. And likely I'll soon be going with her to Philadelphia."

Her eyes narrowed. "Humph," she said. "Eltham. Philadelphia. You're really gettin' fancy, Oney Judge. What makes you think she gonna take *you* to Philadelphia?"

"I told you, I'm her personal girl now."

The hands went on the hips and she strutted about. "Oh. You her *personal* girl now, huh? Well, let me tell you somethin', Miz Personal Girl. You go wif her to Philadelphia and you take your chance and run away."

"Mama!"

"Never you mind. Doan you 'Mama' me. I always knowed what was good for you. You think you got to be her *personal girl* because of the color of your eyes? I worked for years to get you in that house. So you listen. When she take you to Philadelphia, you run, girl. For all you're worth! If she take you, and the way I knows Lady Washington, she won't."

124

"She will." Tears came to my eyes.

"You be up north in Philadelphia," she whispered. "Nobody kin make you come back. You hear?"

I trembled. There was a look in her eyes I couldn't account for. A fire.

"You take that liberty the general fought for. *If* she take you to Philadelphia! You take it for us all!"

"Yes, Mama," I said.

For a full moment she held my gaze. Smoke puffed from the hearth. I coughed. But I could not take my eyes from her, from her turbaned head, her fine face full of pockmarks, her slender shoulders under the raggedy shift.

It was as if she had taken up a hot poker and touched me with it. *You take that liberty.*

"Yes, Mama," I said. All the while knowing I could never do it, and hating myself for the knowing.

I turned then and went out the door.

It was as if Mama had put a fix on me, the idea of running had never come to me before. Why should I run? I was treated well, dressed in fine clothing, given the best of everything to eat. I had a good, warm bed at night. I walked about in an elegant house, where people spoke in soft voices.

125

And now here she was, telling me to run. And look at her! Look at what she'd gotten for her trouble!

I was Lady Washington's personal girl, I told myself. It was just Mama's old jealousy. She wanted to ruin it all for me.

But still, I could not help thinking on it. After two days of having my head so mixed up I was bumping into things, I went to see Old Sinda.

"I think my mama's put a fix on me," I said.

She laughed. She was mixing some remedies on the wooden table in her cabin. Though she was not allowed near the mansion house, she was known for her remedies, which often helped the Negroes when ill. Nobody stopped her from making them.

"Why you think dat?"

"She said if I go to Philadelphia with Lady Washington, I should run away. I've never thought about running, but since she said it, it's all I can think of."

"If your mama could do a fix, she'd fix herself," she said.

"Then, why am I feeling this way?"

She was pounding something evil-smelling in a bowl. "Because she's your mama," she said. "You come back later an' I give you a

126

potion so you becalm yourself. An' it will give you power."

"Power?"

"To go against your mama. Though I think you be crazy, girl. Somebody take me to Philadelphia, I'd run, fer sure."

I went back later for the potion. It was a little bit of whiskey in a pewter cup. I drank it down. I'd never had whiskey.

Oh, it burned. I near choked on it. "Why do men like this terrible brew so?" I asked.

"No white mens ever drink dat," she said. "Whiskey an' gunpowder. Give you power. Becalm the heart."

But Lady Washington did not take me to Philadelphia.

She told me that night that she was taking Sally, who was feeling her old self these days. "I must take her with me one last time," she said. "There is plenty of time for you, Oney."

I must have let my distress show.

"There there, dear," she said. "You may go to Fredericksburg with me and the general tomorrow. We're going to visit his mama."

The general's mother's house in Fredericksburg was behind his sister Betty's. The general and Billy Lee rode along beside the chariot. The general's gray horse, Nelson, had been with him through most of the war, and the general was inordinately fond of him.

Inside, Lady Washington did some crewel-work and some talking. And there I was, having to act like a chair again.

"Betty Lewis is the general's younger sister," she said. "Her husband, Fielding, ruined his fortune and his health in the small-arms factory he had in Fredericksburg. She helped him during the war. They made muskets for Yorktown."

When we visited "Aunt Betty," as I was to call the general's sister, I stayed by Lady Washington's side. I shared in the repast. The general was in another room, talking with Mr. Fielding Lewis, Aunt Betty's husband.

After a while Aunt Betty smiled at me. "Why don't you go outside? The sun is lovely and warm today. There's a cat with new kittens in the stables."

The cat was lying in the sun on the winding brick walk between Aunt Betty's house and that of the general's mother.

The general's mother had a kitchen garden between the houses, and there were still some pumpkins left. I petted the cat. Soon the general came out the back door, and I moved off the walk. He nodded to me

128

and proceeded to go in the back door of his mother's house.

Because it was warm, two windows were open on the bottom floor. In a very few moments I heard voices. First a woman's, strong and demanding. Lady Washington had said the general's mama was seventy-eight years old. I never knew anybody that old. Except maybe Sambo Anderson.

"I have never been so poor!" She was yelling and slamming things.

I gasped. Should I run? Dare I listen? Nobody raised a voice to the general!

"I pay your bills," I heard the deep voice answering. "I pay you thirty pounds a year."

"And you will continue to do so!" she shouted. "And give me any money I need in between. Or I will once again appeal to the government of Virginia for money!"

"You wish to embarrass me." The general's voice again. "And stop badgering Lund for money. He has given you more than two hundred and sixty pounds this year. You know I'll give you my last sixpence to keep you from distress, but never again go to the government of Virginia for a pension."

They must have moved into another room then. The cat had gotten up and started toward the stables. I followed her so the general wouldn't find me lurking about when he came out.

In a few moments he did. From the stable door I saw him, head bowed, hat in hand. Never before had I seen him looking so cast down.

I don't suppose it matters if you're Negro or white, I thought. *If your mama doesn't love you, you've got no color. You've got nothing.* My heart went out to the general as I watched him cover the distance between his mama's and his sister's houses.

And in that moment, in the warm November sun, with the pumpkins shining orange in his mama's garden, and the cat rubbing against my ankles, I felt a oneness with him, even as I laughed at the notion. Me and the general? Suffering the same feelings?

But I knew the oneness could not be denied. And in my heart, in that moment, was born a loyalty to him it would take me years to deny.

CHAPTER THIRTEEN
1783

In the next two years I took example from the general. I went to visit my own mama at least once a month. Even though most of the time she was unkind to me. I brought her small things. A leftover bit of pye or custard, a new shift or skirt I'd made her. Lady Washington had given me permission.

"We must always be good to our mamas," she said, "though they provoke a tempest."

The general and Lady Washington were away a lot in those two years. In Newburgh, in the land of New York; Philadelphia, in the land of Pennsylvania; Princeton, in the land of New Jersey. But I did not go. Old Sally, though half blind, still went with Lady Washington.

I grew taller, not only in height, but in my sense of self. I was well on my way to becoming a woman.

Mama was a long time healing after Yorktown. She was put to work — not to the hoe, but in the weavers' cottage. It was there that I would bring her news of the goings-on at the mansion house. She pretended not to care, indeed she had a sassy answer for everything I said, but I knew she was interested. She loved gossip.

"Little Wash and Nelly live with us now."

"Knew Miz Nelly would pawn 'em off on Lady Washington sooner or later."

"Nobody knows who started the fire in the stables. But Giles and Paris did their best to rescue the horses, though ten were lost."

The dark eyes sought mine, then looked away. "If'n I knew, I wouldn't tell you."

Did she know something? Had it been started by an angry Negro? Yes, they caused trouble on occasion. They broke things, stole things, even ruined crops, but a fire?

"They try to put the blame on Gunner," Mama said. "But he weren't here that night. He out nightwalkin'."

I knew Gunner was trouble. Knew Mama sometimes nightwalked with him.

"Mama, his name is not bespoke in a good light around here. Maybe you should stay away from him. He's a rascal."

"I run wif whoever I please on my own time," she said.

But she would not look at me.

★ ★ ★

In October, Lady Washington came home. She was home for good now. The war was over. The British would be departing from New York in November, she said.

She brought china, fabric, linens, from Philadelphia.

And then, a week after she came home, we had trouble.

Gunner killed somebody.

Nobody knew about it until the men with the long guns came riding up the road and knocked on the door one evening when Lady Washington, Mr. Lund, and his wife were at table.

There was much low talk by Mr. Lund with the men. Then Mr. Lund called for his horse, and they rode to Muddy Hole Farm.

Nathan told me later what happened.

Gunner had been nightwalking to Alexandria. On the way home he met a white man on the road who asked him where he belonged. Gunner refused to answer. The white man tried to tie him up. Gunner grabbed the white man's knife and with "wickedly willful violence," as the men with long guns had said, "killed the white man and was seen in the act by hunters in the vicinity."

133

My heart sank. "Was anybody night-walking with him, Nathan?"

"No."

I was trembling for Mama.

Lady Washington was so distressed that she wrote that day to her husband. Gunner was bound and taken away.

"He wuz always the downrightest fool," Mama said. "What do he expect?"

"Mama, what will happen to him?"

"You a worse fool than he is," she spit out at me. "They kill him. Maybe burn him alive."

"The general would not allow that. Or Lady Washington," I protested.

But she only laughed. "When you gonna learn, girl? First chance they get, they put us aside. An' you no different. Remember that."

The men in Alexandria executed Gunner right before Christmas.

Then, on Christmas Eve, the general came home for good. The house was aglow with candles and decked with greenery. There was a feast being cooked in the kitchen. And, Negro or white, you could feel the peace falling about the place, with the snow outside, which fell quickly and silently and soon closed off the outside world.

On Christmas Day the servants all came up to the house to receive gifts. Rum and shirts for the men. Blankets and shoes for the women. Sweetmeats for the children.

I knew how blessed I was, standing there with the house Negroes, watching the others take the gifts. And I felt guilty, too, especially when mama took hers.

I went to visit her. She was cooking a pot of meat. "Heard the general got money for Gunner."

"Money?" I asked.

"What you think? Gunner be his property. General lost property, he gotta be paid for it. Same's he would lose money if'n he lost you."

She threw the words in my face like a pail of slops. I went back to the mansion house, where I knew I was more than a piece of property.

The long winter that followed, it seemed to be always snowing. For weeks we were snowbound in the elegant house, with fires burning cheerfully in all the rooms and good smells of cooking coming from the kitchen. I played with little Nelly and Wash. I sewed with Lady Washington. The general spent hours in his study, writing letters and planning his spring planting.

I visited Mama. "Mr. Thomas Nelson came to visit, Mama. He was a signer. You know what that means?"

"No, but I 'spect you gonna tell me."

"He signed the Declaration of Independence."

"Lotta good it did us Negroes."

"At Yorktown, Mr. Nelson had the guns turned on his own house because it was a British headquarters. Now he is destitute."

"So is you."

"The general says Mr. Lund is not to send to England for anything he can get on tolerable terms elsewhere."

"If I'da felt that way, I'da been better off. Wouldn't of married your daddy."

"The general received a mantelpiece of brown sienna jasper with three white marble panels from London."

"My, ain't we fancy, knowin' such words."

"The general is paying for the education of his sister Betty's three boys at Fredericksburg Academy."

"General oughta look to his own doorstep. Give his people better vittles."

"His sister, Betty, and her woman friends made cartridges for the soldiers in the war."

"I'd make cartridges myself, if'n I had the paper and lead. Start my own revolution. Right here."

"Mama, don't talk like that. Oh, yes. Mrs. Lund was delivered of another dead child."

"That woman jus' too mean to give life, is all."

CHAPTER FOURTEEN
Winter 1783-Summer 1784

White children have childhoods. Negro slave children don't. If there are moments of joy, afternoons of splashing in a brook, playing "prisoner's base" or a game with clay marbles in the dust, the moment lives forever in the memory because it must. So little joy comes after.

But in the mansion house I lived on the joy of others. I made it mine. Because they made me part of it.

When the snow broke, the gifts started to come for the general. And every time a wagon approached bearing them, we all rushed to see what had been sent.

One day came buckeye nuts from a man with the strange name of Light Horse Harry Lee. Pheasants and partridges came. Linden and lime trees from the governor in the land of New York. A wagonload of the general's wartime papers.

One of the general's old friends from the

war, with the French name of the Marquis de Lafayette, sent some hounds from France. Soon one of the females had a batch of puppies, and I was allowed to fondle them, play with them.

I was part of all the excitement, and the troubles.

The new roof leaked. The planking was still on the windows in the unfinished north room. The new icehouse and greenhouse were being built. The general had to pay for the education of nephews, his brother Sam's sons and his sister's boys. People came to him to borrow money.

For some reason, the pheasants and partridges died. But the deer the general had gotten from England lived. A paddock was built for them. He wanted them tamed. They were gentle creatures, and I fed them bits of dried apple and horse fodder.

Visitors came. So many. Some announced, some by surprise, just riding up the road. People with names like Carter and Lee always seemed to be about.

And I remember the day Margaret Thomas, wife of Billy Lee, came.

The general had paid for her passage from Philadelphia to Alexandria. She was tall and thin and not very well, but she was here. And she was free.

I had never before laid eyes on a Negro woman who was free.

I stared at her until Lady Washington admonished me. I brought her some blankets in the small dependency where she and Billy Lee lived, near the mansion-house servants' quarters.

"How did you get free?" was one of the first questions I asked her.

She was still unpacking, but she made me tea. "Chile, I purchased my own freedom. But there be no work in Philadelphia if you free an' Negro. I had my own garden an' chickens, an' tried to sell eggs an' vegetables. But in the north, white women gots the market for that. Sometimes I peddled oysters an' cakes, but I got sick then, wif this cold in my bones, an' Billy say I shud come here."

"How does it feel to be free?" I asked.

She shrugged. "I been free for near ten years, chile. Tell the truth, I had a warmer bed an' better meals when I was head cook in my master's house. After that I had to worry 'bout myself. An' that's no romp, let me tell you."

Still, I was taken with her. But I was careful not to let anybody know that I visited.

That spring of 1784 many of the general's old war friends came to visit him. They had names like James Monroe, Benjamin Lincoln, John Cadwalader, James Madison, Nathanael Greene, Henry Knox, Anthony Wayne.

It was just a matter of time before they asked for Billy Lee. But he had fallen and broken his knee, and was not running about the house anymore. A young man named Christopher had been put in his stead.

It was my job to escort the visitors to see Billy Lee. So I'd bring them to where he lived with Margaret. I'd knock on the door and call to him, while the important gentlemen, in their high, dusty boots, swords, and tricorn hats, waited outside.

Patiently they would wait. One or two would always have bottles of Madeira. Another, glasses. And Billy Lee would invite them in. And I'd leave.

But not before hearing the loud and glad greetings between them. Not before seeing the hugs. And never before I heard: "Remember, Billy? Remember?"

I'd stand a moment outside the door and listen.

"Remember Monmouth, Billy? When you paraded a corps of valets under that sycamore tree and pulled out your telescope? The British spied *you* on that horse of yours. What was his name?"

"Chinkling," Billy Lee said. "I still gots him."

"Yes. And the British paid their respects to you and Chinkling and your corps of valets with a shot from a six-pounder!"

Everyone laughed. "It cut away, the limbs of the tree and sent your corps scampering. Remember, Billy?"

And Billy Lee, limping and old now, remembered.

Remembering eases the pain. We can choose what we wish to remember and pretend that the things we wish to forget never happened. I remember the day Old Sally died, the summer of 1784, and everyone, Negro and white, witnessed her burial in the slave cemetery.

I remember the coming of the man with the French name. The man who made the general's eyes light up. The Marquis de Lafayette. "Like a son he is to the general," Lady Washington told me. "At the Battle of the Brandywine he fought bravely and was wounded in the leg, but refused to leave the field. The general had to order him to retire. Then the general told the surgeons to treat him as if he were the general's son."

The Marquis came that summer. I was twelve. Old enough to know things I should not speak about. Young enough still to listen behind doors.

The summer evening was like warm creek water against the skin. The smell of Persian jasmine filled the air. On the front piazza Lady Washington's tea table was set, but she was not there. Only the general and the Marquis sat, talking. There came the soft sound of laughter and the strange tone of the Marquis's voice. From where I stood, just around the corner of the piazza, I listened.

"*Mon general,* permit me to propose a plan to you that might become greatly beneficial to the black part of mankind."

"We have discussed this before in letters, Gilbert. I know I promised to listen when we met in person. I am listening."

"Emancipation. Free the enslaved. Your influence, *mon general* cannot be better employed than in inducing the people of America to strengthen their federal union by freeing these people. It is the finishing stroke that is wanting in the temple of liberty."

"Would to God that such a spirit would enter into the minds of the people," the general said.

"You must put it there, *mon general.*"

The general's words came, soft and sad.

"The time is hardly ripe, Gilbert. How is one to work a plantation without Negro hands?"

"With leadership from you, *mon general*, a way will be found. When I make my address to the Virginia House of Delegates, I will put forth my feeling."

"Gilbert, Gilbert, you are like a son to me," came the reply. "I want, more than anything, to free these people. But what will become of them? Some are old and sick. They depend on us for care. Some are children whose parents have died. None can read or write. How can we send them off? And to what?"

There was silence. And then I heard something that changed my whole life.

"I cannot promise you, Gilbert, that your words to the Virginia House of Delegates will be well received. I can promise you that upon my death, my slaves will be freed."

I gasped. Had I heard right? We were to be free upon the general's death? I ran, away from the side of the house, through the lavender summer night. And I held in my heart this secret.

It carried me through the next nine years.

CHAPTER FIFTEEN
Spring 1789

I was going to New York. I was leaving Mount Vernon in the company of Lady Washington.

The general had been elected president. It was a new word for us all. Nobody knew what a president was. In the house the servants had to learn how to say the word. Just like they had to learn how to say "United States of America."

Or "American."

"We are now American," Nathan said to me one day in the kitchen.

"Are we?" Christopher asked. "Are we Negroes American?"

"Yes," Nathan answered, but the answer was weak. It had no legs. It could not walk. It just lay there.

Christopher was just a year or two older than me, straight, with a ready smile and a way of making you feel better, just being around him.

He was acting in Billy Lee's stead as body servant for the general. Billy Lee had started drinking after breaking another leg last year. Now he could scarce walk.

But he'd begged to be taken to New York when the general left with his aides and servants in April.

Everyone knew Billy was in pain as he rode next to the carriage. He got as far as Philadelphia, but there his legs gave out. A note came to Lady Washington from Mr. Biddle in Philadelphia: "I have advised your husband to have Billy Lee sent back to Mount Vernon, but that rascally Billy refuses. I have had Dr. Smith examine him. A steel brace has been made to strengthen his knee. I write to advise you today, madam, that he has made his way to New York to rejoin his master."

All the house servants shook their heads. All knew that if Billy Lee was returned, he would start up with his drinking again.

Now, five weeks after the general had left, Lady Washington was leaving to join him.

It was the last day of May. The plantation was in fine fettle under Mr. George Augustine, the general's nephew. No more Mr. Lund. He and his wife had moved to their own place a short distance away.

For all her praying, they had lost a third

child. I wondered: If God wasn't kind to those who prayed on their knees to Him every day, how could He be kind to the rest of us?

No sense wondering about God, though. There were too many people I didn't understand who had to be worried about first.

But why worry on a beautiful spring morning? I had four new dresses, half a dozen new neckerchiefs, three new mobcaps, two pairs of shoes, and my very own cloak of purple wool.

We would leave tomorrow. The general's nephew Bob Lewis was escorting us. I was on my way to the quarters to say good-bye to Old Sinda and to my mama.

First person I met on my way there was Christopher. He darted out from behind the greenhouse. "Psst, Oney."

"What are you sneaking up on me for, Christopher?"

"We gotta talk."

I stopped on the lane to the quarters. He stood in front of me, a head taller. "Talk, Christopher."

"Is everybody gonna hate me if I get sent for?"

"You're so full of fear, Christopher. You see a haint behind every tree. Sent for where? Who's gonna send for you?"

"The general. In New York. If Billy Lee can't serve him anymore, he'll send for me. I'm scared, Oney."

"Scared to go to New York?"

"No. Scared they'll all hate me if I take Billy Lee's place."

"I took Old Sally's place, didn't I?"

"But she died."

I sighed. "Nobody's gonna hate you, Christopher. Anyway, you have to do your job even if they do. We Negroes can't worry about what others think of us. That's for white folk to do. Now, get out of my way. I've got to go and make some visits in the quarters before I leave."

He shook his head. "Wish I was like you, Oney. You're afeared of nuthin.' "

But I was. Only, what I feared I couldn't put words on. I feared that the general would die and we would all be free. Oh, I wanted freedom. I'd heard all about it from Lady Washington over the years. I'd grown up hearing about it.

It was something men died for. Bled for. Froze for. Starved for.

And I'd learned about it from Margaret Thomas, Billy Lee's wife, who'd died last year. She'd said that as an expert mistress of the needle, I could earn a living on my own.

An excitement flowed through me. No, I

did not want the general to die. I did not want to run away. But New York was the North. For the first time in my life I felt that anything could happen.

"So, you goin'."

"Yes, Mama. Tomorrow. We leave tomorrow."

Her hair was white now, her face lined, her body bent, and her face pockmarked. She looked spent. But she wasn't that old.

"So you gots what you always wanted, finally."

"Yes, Mama."

"Well, girl, if you ever come back here again, I'll kill you."

Oh, Lordy, why did I come? To say goodbye. To have her good words. Not this. Not the old envy, when I knew I might never see her again. Was this all she could give me?

Her words were spoken in a harsh whisper. She picked up a knife from the old table. She held it, pointed at me.

"You ever come back to this place, I'll kill you, Oney Judge. 'Cause you deserve to die if you doan take your freedom in New York."

She set down the knife. I stared at her. She drew her worn shawl about her shoulders and looked at the knife on the table.

I ran to her. I hugged her. "Oh, Mama," I said. "You do love me. You do."

After that I went to see Old Sinda.

There was no counting years with Old Sinda. God had lost count with her. But she still made her remedies, did her fixes. "Long time ago I tells you you gonna be free," she said in her slow, cracked voice. "An' you gonna be, chile."

"Sinda, why does everyone expect this from me? And not any of the others who are going?"

"I doan 'spect. I knows," she said.

Then she put her thin, gnarled hands on my shoulders. "Maybe not yet. Not fer a while."

"I suppose we'll all be free after a while, Sinda," I said. It was the closest I'd come to revealing my secret.

She shook her head no. "Not Old Sinda. I be dead. So will lotsa others. But you, you be free first, afore de time."

"What time?"

She shook her head, casting off my question. "It ain't gonna be easy, bein' free. But it be good. Now, Old Sinda give you some remedies."

She gave me green cockleburs made into a poultice for skin ailments, cockroach tea for coughs, earthworm tea mixed with lard for rashes, and some basil.

"What does this do?"

"Protect you against hexes. Doan know but what dose peoples in New York do hexes. Can't have you hexed up dere."

She gave me graveyard dirt in a small sack. "Put some in your shoes, in case you walk on evil. An' you be careful not to walk over any evil root buried under de doorstep of dat house in New York."

"I won't, Sinda."

"An' you 'member, you doan ever carry out ashes on Friday."

"It isn't my job to carry out ashes."

"An' never carry a hoe or spade into de house. Or mend clothes while dey on a body. An' if you start off on dis trip an' anybody have to come back 'cause dey forgot sumptin', you 'member to make an x in de road before you turn around."

I kissed her, crying. I promised her everything.

CHAPTER SIXTEEN
Spring-Fall 1789

Lady Washington was anxious.

"I don't know what I'm supposed to do as wife of the president," I heard her saying as she leaned into the general's shoulder on the carriage ride to the New York house. "Am I supposed to hide from people? Go out and meet them? Tell me."

"We will find out as we go along," he told her. "It will be all right. Everything you do will be all right."

I thought how wonderful it would be if someone told me that everything would be all right too.

After that Lady Washington was anxious no more.

I was sure to step over the threshold of the house on Cherry Street, so I wouldn't touch any evil root buried under the doorstep.

It was a grand house, facing Franklin Square. Brick, large and commodious. It was a block from the East River, and looking that way, you could see the water dotted with the sails of boats.

There was an excitement in New York. An air of something always just about to happen. I heard someone say it was the leading port in the country.

We settled in. My room was on the topmost floor. From there I could really see the river, the masts of the big boats that came and went, carrying goods to and from the city.

Those masts signaled to me. They said something to me. I just was not quite sure what.

Seven of us had been brought from Mount Vernon. Sall and Caroline, Hercules and his son, Richmond, who would help him in the kitchen because Nathan had been left behind to cook at home. Myself and Giles and Billy Lee. Although, within a day Billy Lee had to go back home. He could scarce hobble about anymore. And he was drinking again. Within a fortnight Christopher came.

He was the one who stood up to the white servant woman Mary, one of five white servants the Washingtons had employed in New York.

Mary thought she was over us all, Negro and white. She was a large, hatchet-faced, sour woman who could have used a fix from Old Sinda. And she ordered us all about, all except Hercules. She tried with Hercules, but he threw apples at her.

Anyone who knew Hercules knew that throwing apples was one step short of burning sugar. If he burned sugar, he was ready to quit. Apples were a warning.

Lucky for us all, the apples were enough to scare old Hatchet Face. Then Christopher arrived.

That very night he was in the kitchen fetching a pot of tea for the general. He had just put a white linen napkin over it when Mary came in.

"Why do you have to put a fresh linen napkin on that tray, boy?" Mary asked. "I can't keep this house in fresh linen napkins."

Everyone in the kitchen held their breath as Christopher turned to her. "My name isn't 'boy.' It's Christopher," he said.

"I don't care what your name is. You'll answer when spoken to."

"I answer only to the general and his lady," Christopher said.

"You'll answer to me! I am in charge of all you servants."

"The day you're in charge of me is the day I turn myself over to Beelzebub," Christopher said. And he strode past her, out of the kitchen.

That was the end of it. Until the next time Mary tried to hold sway over us.

Lady Washington liked to oversee the making of the bread dough every evening. All the Negroes from Mount Vernon knew that. At home she came into the kitchen every night before bed and tested the feel of the dough before it was covered.

At home the dough had been made by Nathan. Here it was made by Richmond. One evening Mary came into the kitchen and asked why the dough was not yet covered for the night.

"Lady Washington likes to test it first with her own hands," Caroline said.

"Nonsense," Mary said briskly. "The lady of the house should not be bothered with such things. Cover the dough, Caroline."

"No, ma'am. I waits for Lady Washington."

Mary turned to Sall and got the same answer. Then to me. "Not until Lady Washington tests it," I said.

And so we waited in the kitchen, in silence, all of us, and also Hercules and Richmond. The minutes ticked by. We could hear voices and laughter from the main part of the house. Then finally came Lady Washington's footsteps in the dog run that separated the kitchen from the house.

In that moment Mary stepped forward and covered the dough loaves with napkins.

Lady Washington came into the kitchen. If she suspected anything, with us all standing around like pigs in the rain, she said nothing. "Why is the bread dough covered?" she asked.

The Mount Vernon Negroes did not answer. Mary did. "I have put it to rise for the night, Lady Washington."

"But my servants know I test it every evening. Haven't they told you this?"

Lady Washington looked at us, from one to the other, and saw the answer in our silent, downcast faces. Then she looked at me. "Oney, uncover the bread dough, please."

I did so, gladly.

Then she performed her little ceremony. She held out her hands. "Richmond, the flour," she said. And he stepped forward and dusted her hands with flour. She thanked him and, one loaf at a time, picked up the dough, weighing it in her hands, tossing it up and down. "Perfect," she said. "Oney, cover the dough and come with me to my bedchamber. I am tired."

I did so. As I passed Mary on the way out I could not help but give her a look that would freeze a holly bush in December.

Lady Washington asked me nothing about the incident, and I offered no information.

Still, I knew a line had been drawn on the brick floor of the kitchen. But that was not the end of it.

Lady Washington had decided she would have a tea every Friday. These teas were called levees and were open to any ladies of consequence who might put in an appearance.

The trouble came when I was to sit in at the teas. I was to serve. "Madam," Mary suggested, "wouldn't it be proper to keep the Negro servants in the kitchen?"

"In the kitchen?" Lady Washington asked.

"Yes, madam. Out of sight."

I stood there, with a tea tray in hand, acting like a chair.

"If I want Oney to serve at my teas, she will do so," Lady Washington said. "She is like a daughter to me."

"Madam," Mary said, "it is not proper."

"I will decide what is proper and what is not proper," Lady Washington said sweetly. "Now, go and get the scones."

I loved her for that. And when I told the

others in the kitchen, they did too. "She said we are to be treated right," I told them. "That we have been with her and the general a long time. And are of value."

In the corner of the kitchen, getting a tray of cherry bounce for the general, I heard Christopher mumble, "I wonder how valuable, is all."

The general was dying.

It was only a month since we'd come. I looked out the fine square window in the front of the house and saw Giles and Christopher spreading straw down on the cobblestone street to keep the sound of passing carriages dull, so they would not disturb the ailing general. The doctors had come and gone, one of them the old faithful Dr. Craik. It had started with a fever, then the general had a tumor on his thigh and it had to be lanced.

White servants were whispering the word *cancer*. I took off my shoes when I went to my third-floor room, so as not to make any sound to disturb him. There was a pall over the house. Wash and Nelly were kept belowstairs when they returned from lessons. Thank heaven, Lady Washington had managed to get Little Wash into a school with seven other boys under a Mr. Murdoch. And

Nelly at the fashionable Mrs. Graham's on Maiden Lane. Their chatter wouldn't bother him during the day.

What would happen if he died?

A thrill of fear ran through me because I knew.

We would be free, all the Negro servants here and at Mount Vernon.

But I could not think on the word *free* as having anything behind it. I was sure that if I looked, behind it there would be nothing but a great darkness.

Then I had to remind myself that I was the only Negro servant who knew the general was going to free us upon his death, and now that secret burned inside me as if I had a fever.

I should tell someone. But who? Certainly all Negro slaves knew that the death of the master meant change, and change was never good for slaves. The death of a master usually meant you would be sold.

As the days went on, the street in front was now roped off to keep away noise. Delivery people came to the kitchen door with fresh fish, vegetables, milk, and butter. "Any word of the president?" they would ask.

We were told to say he was middling well.

It was June. I was allowed my time off, and Lady Washington encouraged me to get out of the house. "You are so young, child. Walk. Get some fresh air," she said.

So I walked to the wharf at the end of the street. There was a small park, where nannies took babies. I sat on a bench under the trees and watched the frantic goings and comings of the men loading and unloading the ships, checking items off on paper, yelling orders to the Negroes who loaded them. I minded the crying of the gulls, a new sound to me. I watched them floating on the air overhead, free, so free.

I smelled the sea air. I saw merchants in silk breeches, meeting, walking, inspecting the incoming cargo. I saw the fancy carriages that waited for them, with liveried Negroes holding the horses' reins.

There is a world beyond Mount Vernon, I told myself. *A whole world I have never seen. And if the general dies, I must not be afraid to embrace it.*

Would Lady Washington take us back to Mount Vernon if he died? Being free in Virginia would certainly be more difficult than being free in New York.

Should I tell the others what I knew so they, too, would be prepared?

One day while I was sitting on a bench in the park, mulling these things over, I saw Christopher approaching. Then he stopped to speak to another Negro man. I saw him hand the man a piece of folded parchment.

And it came to me. Christopher could write!

He waved, then came to sit next to me on the bench. "A friend of yours?" I asked.

"It behooves us to make as many friends in the outside world as we can," he said.

I smiled. "To what end?"

He leaned forward, elbows on his knees. "Come now, Oney. You want the same thing as I do. Admit it."

"What?" I asked innocently.

He scuffed the dirt with the toe of his shoe. "I talked to Old Sinda before I left too. I know what you want. Same's we all want. Freedom."

A warmth spread through me. "If I admit that to you, will you admit to me that you can write?"

"Course I can write. Nathan taught me. And I can read, too. An' the first thing I aim to do when I get the chance here in New York is take my freedom."

"You mean *run?*"

His grin was sassy. "Tha's what I mean, Oney. You mean you ain't thought of it?"

"None of us may have to. Can you keep a secret if I tell you?"

"You know I can."

"The general is going to free us all upon his death. I overheard him telling the Marquis that when he visited."

He whistled. It was a low and pure sound. "So we may be free sooner than we 'spect, then."

"Yes. I just didn't know whether I should tell the others or not. Prepare them."

He stood up. He looked around. "The mist would be hanging low over the Potomac now," he said.

"Yes."

"In the marshes the peepers be singin'."

"Yes."

"The coves of the river be filled with yellow and white water lillies. And the wild grapevines be growin' strong around the water's edge."

"Oh, Christopher, don't."

"You miss it, Oney?"

"I can't bear to think on it."

He leaned toward me. "Then, that's why you gotta tell the others if he dies. Give 'em a chance to leave. Here in New York. And not go back. Takin' your freedom in Virginia is like pullin' away from your mama's arms."

"Yes," I said again.

He patted my shoulder. "I hafta get back now. Thanks."

I was glad to be able to tell somebody.

Glad to be able to unburden myself. But the general did not die. He languished on his sickbed all summer. Important men came and went. But he recovered.

Autumn came. He got out of bed. I felt a sense of relief.

And then I felt guilty over that, too. What kind of a person was I, that I was relieved not to have to be set free?

My mama hadn't had the privileges I'd had, yet she'd known in an instant that day to go with the British when they came to the wharf of Mount Vernon. It hadn't taken her but a minute to decide she wanted to be free. I felt ashamed.

And then for a while I forgot all about being free. I and all the other Mount Vernon Negroes had a new worry. It seemed as if Hercules was in some kind of trouble. Either that or he was going mad.

CHAPTER SEVENTEEN

We discovered the strange behavior of Hercules on a weekday in November, when Lady Washington and I had returned from one of her daily carriage rides around Manhattan.

The general had left a few days before, in a carriage drawn by four white horses, with his secretaries and servants, including Christopher. They were off on a trip to New England.

Every day Lady Washington rode fourteen miles in her carriage around New York.

I did not know what to think of the place. It was, at once, home to the very rich and the very poor. Its market people sometimes spoke in a strange language. Lady Washington said it was Dutch. She also said the city had two disastrous fires in the war. Hundreds of places of business and houses had been charred to ruins, and some of them were not yet repaired. The British had overrun the city when they occupied it for seven years.

We passed one or two houses, still in ruins, that had a large *R* painted on their half-open front doors.

"That's for 'rebel,'" Lady Washington told me. "The British did that." Lady Washington would miss nothing in her daily ride. She made Paris, who was driving, pass every point of interest, every day. She loved the "hubbub of Manhattan," as she called it. We must go by the grog houses, the warehouses, the enticing shop windows. And she kept a notebook handy to mark down her observations.

We must go on the narrow cobblestone of Wall Street to Federal Hall, where the general was sworn in as president. Past Saint Paul's Chapel, where he and the Congress had gone afterward. Past Fraunces Tavern, where he said good-bye to his men after the war.

"Look," she would say, "look." And she would grab my hand as she pointed something out to me, and sometimes giggle like a girl. I felt very close to her in these times.

"I wonder what small town those people come from," she'd say, pointing at some wagons being driven by cattle, coming in from the country. Or, "Look, there is a scissor sharpener, Oney. I must take note of the street corner and send Giles or Paris to fetch him to the house. Oh, we're on Broadway. No surprise at the activity. See the vendors hawking firewood and hot corn? And look, Oney dear. There is our new house."

We looked. "It's the old Macomb mansion," she whispered as we passed, "and is reputed as being the grandest house in New York."

I peered at the square four-story building as we passed. Some pigs were routing after garbage on the street in front of it. Workmen were repairing it. I caught a glimpse of stables being built behind it. "The servants will live in one of those new buildings out back," she told me. "But you, Oney, will be in our house, as always."

I felt a glow of belonging.

"It may cost as much as twenty cords of firewood to heat it the month of December alone," she said. "Oh dear, I hope people will not think we are being extravagant."

I told her I thought people wouldn't think such. "I hear nothing but good things about you and the general from everyone," I told her. "Wherever I go. And people are so jealous of me because I am part of your household."

She hugged me, like I was her own. And the feel of her arms remained around me on the ride home. I think we became closer that day than we'd ever been.

And then, arriving home, we saw another carriage in Franklin Square, with a Negro couple bringing portmanteaus up the steps to the president's mansion.

"Oh, oh," Lady Washington said. And she near stumbled as Paris helped her down. "Oh, it's my girls, my other granddaughters!"

And she ran up the steps and into the house. I sat in the carriage. Dark was coming on. The November sky threatened snow. Men were lighting the oil lamps on the street corners. And I never felt so abandoned in my life.

At first I could scarce recognize Eliza, who'd been the baby I'd minded for Master Jackie years ago. She appeared like a woman, wearing an English gown of salmon-colored taffeta, which gave advantage to her figure. And she, with a full bosom already, not even wearing the proper daytime neckerchief for traveling.

Martha, whom they called Patsy, was twelve and was still a little girl. There was much kissing and hugging, of course. "How is your dear mama, and your steppapa, Dr. Stuart?" Lady Washington asked.

Eliza rolled her eyes. "Hope Park is hopeless. If Mama hadn't consented to this visit, I would have run away. Oh, Grandmama, you must let us go to the theater. And have teas for us. To think that my grandpapa is president of the United States and I live on a farm with nothing for miles around!"

"It isn't much more exciting here," Lady Washington told her. "But sometimes I feel like I am a prisoner. There is only so much I can do as the wife of the president without inviting censure."

Eliza reached for a bonbon from a bowl on a nearby table and caught sight of me. "Oney. It is you, isn't it?"

"Yes," I said.

"Well, don't you curtsy anymore?"

I dropped a small curtsy to her.

"Well, fetch a tray of tea and cakes for us. I do so miss the servant who came with us. She took sick at Elizabethtown and we had to leave her."

It became clear to me in a second. Eliza was setting herself up as mistress, and I as Negro servant. The last time I had seen her, she had been a child. We'd played with dolls together.

But we were no longer children, and lines

had to be drawn. White people always did this to Negro children they had grown up with.

I ordered the tea from the kitchen. She had dropped into a chair. "Oney, take off my shoes and rub my feet. They are absolutely frozen."

I knelt and took off Eliza's shoes and rubbed her feet. "I'll fetch a warmed brick from the kitchen," I said.

Then, as I disappeared, I heard her asking: "Grandmama, who *is* that crazed-looking Negro man outside, marching up and down in those absurd clothes? Does he work here?"

"We have no crazed Negroes working for us," I heard Lady Washington answer.

"He looks as mad as George the Third, who I hear they have in a straitjacket these days. Come to the window, Grandmama, and see."

When I returned, the three of them were at the window.

"Oh dear," Lady Washington was saying. "It is Hercules." She turned to me. "Look, Oney."

I peered over her shoulder. And sure enough, there on the wooden walk out front was Hercules, strutting up and down, wearing the most ridiculous attire.

I had heard that he walked about sometimes in a dandy's clothing. I had never seen
him in it. Now I saw.

On his feet were pointed slippers of red
silk. With heels. On his legs were silken hose
of white. His breeches were of yellow silk,
his coat a nightmarish color of blue and
green, patterned after the frock coat of the
general's, with gold lace at the shoulders
and pewter buttons on the blue facings.

On his head was a tricorn hat with two
feathers in it.

Lady Washington put one hand over her
mouth and the other to her heart. "What is
he about? He will certainly bring disgrace
down upon this house. Oney, go and bring
him inside. I think he may be drunk."

"Hercules! Hercules!"

He did not answer, so I called him by the
name the children had called him back at
Mount Vernon.

"Uncle Harkness!"

He turned, saw me, waved, and smiled. I
ran to him. "Uncle Harkness, what are you
doing out here?"

"Walkin'," he said.

"But you're going nowhere."

"That's why I'm walkin'."

Was he speaking in riddles?

"I's gettin' myself known hereabouts in this city of New York," he said. "So I can go somewhere. Soon."

"Known?"

"Yes." He nodded solemnly and pointed to the street. "See the way those people in the carriages wave to me? They know me. I'm Hercules. I'm the president's dandy."

"But why are you wearing those clothes?"

He put his hands on the facings of the fancy frock coat. "These be fine feathers, don't they?"

"Oh yes, Hercules. Very fancy. But Lady Washington has sent me out to ask you why you are dressed this way. She thought you were drunk."

He leaned closer to me. "I gots plans," he said.

"Plans?"

"Yes, I save my money and buy these clothes. And when I buy 'em, I get to know the people where I'm buyin'. And I got now associates."

My eyes widened. "Associates?"

"Yes, missy. The people I buy from. The people who stop to talk to me because I be the president's dandy. They be my associates. Important for a fellow to have associates. Friends who can help him when he need it."

What was he trying to tell me? "Hercules, where do you get the money to buy these clothes?" I touched the cloth of his coat sleeve. "It's very elegant."

"I sells slops from the kitchen. I been doin' that since we got here. No chance to do such at Mount Vernon. But here, everybody want food from the kitchen of the president. It only gets thrown out, what's left, don't it?"

The words started to make sense to me. What a smart plan!

"I been with that man for years and years, Oney," he said. "I serve him faithful. No reason why I can't sell slops from the kitchen."

"No," I said.

He laughed. "I goes to walk outside the Fighting Cock, near Whitehall Slip, where the rich mens meet. I goes to the Collect. You know the Collect?"

"I know it's a pond," I said.

"All around it there be breweries, potteries, tanneries, and ropeworks. Lotsa ordinary people. I talk to them, too. I got me a whole string of friends already, rich and poor. To help me when the time comes."

"What time is that, Hercules?"

"Why," he said as if I should know, "my time to run, Oney Judge. My time to run."

I nodded. I tried not to show my surprise. *Hercules was planning to run.*

The general's beloved cook! Had he always felt like this? Or was it the move to New York?

And I had no plans. None.

"Let's go back inside," I said gently. "And be careful about strutting about in front of the house, Hercules. Lady Washington's granddaughter Eliza is here. And she's very high toned."

CHAPTER EIGHTEEN
Winter 1789-Spring 1790

I convinced Hercules to stay away from the front of the house, and even from Franklin Square, in his dandy clothes. Surely if he didn't, Eliza would make trouble for him.

So he took his walks elsewhere. But I was taken aback. Two of the most important people in the household had clever notions about becoming free. And I didn't.

What would the general do without Hercules and Christopher?

One evening when the general and Lady Washington were having a dinner party, one of the lady guests caught fire, and Christopher leaped forward and put it out.

It happened so quickly. The lady was wearing tall ostrich feathers in her hair, which was piled about a foot high. The feathers caught fire under the lighted chandelier. Christopher dashed forward with a towel and smothered the flames. He was praised for his quick actions.

Christopher was never far from the general. Always watching from a short distance away to ward off danger or unpleasantness. I could not believe he would ever leave.

The girls, Eliza and Patsy, went home after a week, and I was ever so grateful. Lady Washington sent a white servant with them. Eliza had me running to do her bidding the whole time she was visiting. Fetch a cup of tea. See that her dress was ironed. Fix her hair. Once or twice I looked to Lady Washington, but there was no help forthcoming. She acted as if it were not happening.

When Eliza left, Lady Washington turned to me for companionship again. At first I was put out. Then I thought: *But they are her grandchildren, her kin. Do you expect to come before them in her esteem?*

I did not.

Besides, there was no time to pout. We were packing again. We moved to the Macomb house in February, in a snowstorm. And true to Lady Washington's promise, though the other Negro servants lived in the dependencies out back and had to rush to and fro in the cold, I lived on the third floor in a cozy room with my own fireplace. Wood was brought in twice a day for my fire.

I was given the warmest of blankets, the

best of food. The house was elegant and overlooked the Hudson River, and at any time of day you could see ships with billowing sails floating by. I became accustomed to the sound of the seagulls.

There were fine Turkish carpets on the floor, wallpaper with great scenes painted on it. In daytime the sun bounced off the water and shone in the house. At night the rooms were lighted with whale-oil lamps.

Lady Washington had a quilted petticoat made for me, a flannel underskirt. I was given new, strong shoes and warm hose.

Why would I want to be free, wandering on the howling cold streets, wondering where I would work and live?

When the weather cleared, Mrs. Abigail Adams came to call. She was the wife of the vice president, and Lady Washington introduced me. I accompanied Lady Washington to church, to social calls, even to the theater! I had never been to the theater! Chandeliers hung from the pitched roof, casting magnificent light. But when the play started, they were dimmed and only the candles in glass holders at the rim of the stage glowed. The play was *Constant Couple*. Lady Washington and I sat in a special box, and everyone stood as she entered. Oh, it was so exciting!

Then, in March, Thomas Jefferson came.

The house was aflutter. He was just back from Paris. And he brought gifts, books for the general, a bolt of yellow taffeta for Lady Washington, who most always wore black.

"How do I address you?" he said as he took the general's hand. "I hear John Adams wants people to call you His High Mightiness."

The two men stood facing each other in the east parlor. "Mr. President will be fine," the general said, smiling.

I liked Mr. Jefferson. He was to be secretary of state. I did not know what that meant, but it sounded like a fine title to me. I liked him even more when I heard him say that he could not be secretary of state until after his daughter Martha's wedding. How lucky Martha was to have such a father!

Spring came. And then word that we would soon be moving again. The new capital would be in Philadelphia!

Word buzzed through the house and the dependencies out back. Philadelphia! All the Negro servants knew what that meant.

In Philadelphia they did not countenance slavery.

In Philadelphia there were Quakers working to free the slaves.

Christopher told me this: "There be a law in Pennsylvania that adult slaves brought north for six months be set free. The general could lose us if he keeps us in Philadelphia six months."

"But he won't allow that," I said. "He's too smart for that, isn't he?"

Christopher shrugged.

But before we moved to Philadelphia in the fall, we had to go back to Mount Vernon. Mayhap the general was already acting on the law, bringing us back south because we'd already been up north so long.

And mayhap he just missed Mount Vernon — his bed, which was more than six feet long; his old friends; his horse, Nelson, who had carried him through the war; and the meals he would eat once there, the roasted pig and fowl, the fresh peas, lettuce, and cucumbers from Mount Vernon's gardens.

I dreaded going home. Mama would be so disappointed because I had not taken my freedom. And Mount Vernon tugged at the heart and made one a child again.

On the day we left, a package was delivered for the general. It was from Paris, France, from the Marquis.

It sat on a table in the front parlor, awaiting the general's return from meeting with Congress. I felt drawn to it. When nobody was looking, I picked it up and held it.

Imagine! It had come from Paris, from the Marquis. It had come across the ocean on a ship!

When the general returned home, he was so happy to get it. He opened it immediately.

Inside was a large key, a black-and-white sketch, and a note from the Marquis. "What is it?" Martha asked.

"The key to the Bastille," the general said. "The prison the people tore down. And this is a sketch of the people in the act."

He put the key on the sideboard. I sneaked into the room later and looked at it. And I knew that it was an omen, something Old Sinda would call a sign. And that it was not meant for the general. It was meant for me.

The key to a prison, sent to remind me that I was still in a prison. Sent to make me ask, *When will you tear down the walls and go free?*

CHAPTER NINETEEN
Fall–Winter 1790

Christopher must have been right in what he said about the law in the land of Pennsylvania, because Lady Washington and the general stopped in Philadelphia for four days before going home. But we servants were sent directly on to Virginia.

I rode in a carriage with Christopher and the general's nephew Bob Lewis. Our trip was long. Outside Richmond we rode past flat, muddy tobacco fields. Then we came upon the banks of the Elizabeth River. There we saw wagon after wagon filled with what appeared to be skeletons.

"What are they?" I touched Christopher's arm.

I saw him and Bob Lewis exchange glances. "Those are the bones of the slaves who ran to the British in the war," Lewis said. "I hear they waited on the banks of this river to board ships for freedom in England."

I just stared at him. He went back to

reading his newspaper. I looked at Christopher.

"The boats never came," Christopher told me. "They starved here on the banks of the river. Somebody loaded their bodies into these wagons and just left them. Never even bothered to bury them."

I shuddered, closed my eyes, leaned against Christopher, and thought of Mama.

There was no washing it away, no running from it. Mount Vernon was home. Once there, Christopher shed his red-and-white livery, Hercules put away his fancy silk suit, and I got into my cotton skirt and chemise.

It was September, one of the loveliest months in Virginia. The leaves on the trees were still green, but there was a touch of autumn in the evenings. The mist that gathered over the River of Swans mornings and nights had a winter bite to it.

Soon Lady Washington and the general returned. Soon the mallard ducks flew upriver, past the mansion house, and one could hear the sound of Sambo Anderson's fowling piece piercing the air. Sambo must be older than any African god by now, but he still hunted.

The sounds and smells and gentle daily rhythm of life on the plantation lulled me into being a child again. I went to the quarters to see old friends. I fed the deer in the paddock, the horses in the barn. I brought sugar to old Nelson. I stood on the wharf and watched One-Handed Charles fish. I watched Hercules make blancmange in the kitchen and scraped the bowl with my finger, tasting the sweetness.

I went to see Mama.

"So, you still here."

"Yes," I said.

"You be a fool, Oney Judge." She was doing some weaving. She didn't even have to go to the weavers' cottage. She had her own loom in her place.

"The right time has not come yet, Mama," I told her.

"Right time never come. You gotta make it right."

I gave her my gifts. A new warm blanket from Lady Washington. A flannel petticoat I had stitched myself. Some candied fruit from Hercules. And seven shillings.

She took the money. "Where you get this?"

"Eliza and Patsy visited in New York. Eliza wore me down so much the general gave me money for abiding her bossiness."

She nodded solemnly. "You watch yourself wif that Eliza. She bound to show you who's boss."

"She already has, Mama. I pay no never-mind to her. Now, how have you been keeping?"

She laughed. "Like a barrel of old pickles. Tough and sour."

I saw that her bed was covered with burlap sacks. She could use the new soft blanket. "We go to Philadelphia from here, Mama. The new president's home is in Philadelphia. The city is full of abolitionists."

"Well, you best get a remedy from Old Sinda, then, so you doan catch it."

I smiled. "No, Mama. Abolitionists are people. People who are against slavery. I think I'll have a better chance of taking my freedom in Philadelphia."

Her dark eyes were unbelieving. She thought I was lying, putting her off.

She was right. Only, I was not lying and putting her off. I was lying and putting off myself.

Inside the mansion house every chair seemed to hold out its arms to me. The clocks did not tick, they spoke to me. The twilight whispered to me. I understood what the frogs were saying in the marshes. The new timothy grass the general had planted welcomed my bare feet. The silver service on the sideboard in the dining room threw back my own face, older, sassier, and satisfied.

The general was up at first light every day, riding his twenty-four-mile circuit around his farms. I accompanied Lady Washington to the henhouse, the larder, the icehouse, the greenhouse. The head gardener, Johann Ehlers, had an abundance of lima beans and artichokes and other fresh vegetables for us. He put them in my basket.

I quickly fell back into my old ways, sewing in the mornings with the other seamstresses, listening to the gossip about the people at the place, visiting Old Sinda on the sly.

But we were to leave in November, before winter made the roads bad for travel. The trees turned, then the leaves fell. The red berries on the dogwood trees were already bright scarlet. The new ivy around the icehouse was turning. Flocks of wild geese were flying overhead in the gray skies, calling, calling. Logs burned brightly in every fireplace.

Old Sinda gave me some advice. "Hoppin' John — black-eyed peas, rice, an' ham boiled together an' eaten on New Year's Day — bring a good year," she said.

"Yes, Sinda."

She gave me a new bag of goofer dust.

"Fer de trip. Keep it wif you. I gots bad feelins 'bout dis trip."

On the way to Philadelphia in November, our coach was twice overturned. I was traveling with Lady Washington, little Wash, and Nelly. The coachman had been drinking, and the wheels slipped on wet leaves. The first time it was righted in a few minutes, though the general, on horseback, looked worried. The second time the general was in an outrage. He made the coachman ride in one of the wagons with the trunks. He put Giles to the reins.

I thought, *It is an omen, a sign.* And then I thought: *Old Sinda's bag of goofer dust saved us.*

Philadelphia, they said, was a town full of Quakers dressed in gray who never stopped harping about the evils of slavery.

They also said that the elegance of the ladies' clothing, the gaudiness of the carriages, the elaborate parties, and the rowdy dance halls and theaters would make even those who had seen the royal court surprised.

"These Quakers," I heard the general complain one day. "They cannot live without our Southern crops, yet they pretend scorn for the peculiar institution that supplies them."

That "peculiar institution" was, of course, slavery.

And the general did not like Quakers, Lady Washington confided to me. "During the war they drove him to distraction with their notions of peace. They do not believe in fighting."

I expected to see Quakers, like boll weevils, all over. I saw not a one of them.

The house on Market Street was brick, with three stories and dormers on top. I soon discovered that behind the dormers were cunning rooms with slanted walls and windows that looked out on the rooftops of the city.

I begged a room of my own up there.

"Too far away from me," Lady Washington said.

"In the event of fire, you'll never get out," from the general. But finally they allowed it.

I had a bed with a fine quilt, a small dressing table, rag rugs on the floor, and a fireplace. The room, it turned out, was right above Lady Washington's bedchamber. All she had to do when she needed me was tap her ceiling with a cane or a broomstick.

The other Negro servants, and even some of the white, would have to sleep above the washhouse in back, above the stable, or in the cellar under the kitchen. There were so many servants that some even had to make do with sleeping in the smokehouse.

All was confusion at first, of course, as we settled in. Thank heavens, Mary from New York had not come with us. The white servants who were hired treated us kindly.

We had a fine Christmas. Next door lived Robert Morris, whose house the general was using. The Morrises were very rich, and Nelly soon made friends with their daughter, Maria. Soon another girl joined their circle, Elizabeth Bordley. Her father had an esteemed job with the Bank of the United States.

In no time at all, both girls were in and out of the house, inviting Nelly on sleigh rides, to skating parties, dances, socials, teas.

Of course, Nelly would rather play than study.

Little Wash, at nine, was to go to the Academy of Philadelphia. Nelly had tutors, but Lady Washington had to stand over her to make her study.

I knew the schedule by heart, I heard them arguing over it so much. Monday it was French; Wednesdays and Fridays, grammar lessons and dialogues; Tuesdays and Thursdays, geography and music.

Saturday it was Latin. And more music. I

remember Nelly crying at the pianoforte while Lady Washington stood over her. Crying and blubbering and saying, even while she pounded the keys: "You spoil Wash. You let him get away with everything. But you stand over me with a ruler!"

"Girls do not have an easy life," Lady Washington would say gently. "It may appear to be so. But in the end, dear Nelly, the weight of the world rests on our shoulders. We must be strong to stand behind our men. I will not have you become an affected, trifling Miss of the Town."

Who could argue with the wife of the president of the United States? Nelly could, and did. All she wanted to do was become an affected, trifling Miss of the Town.

There was many a slammed door, many a shout from her, much sobbing. She would run to the general when he came home.

"Grandpapa, why must I be treated so? Why is Grandmama so harsh with me?" She had no awe of him.

The general would hold her, pat her head, say something soothing, then the man who had bested the whole British army would retreat to his library.

And soon there would be another visit from the mantua maker, the lady who brought bolts of silk and taffeta and made dresses. And Nelly was mollified and would promise to do her Latin and French.

And so a list would be made up for new fittings for Nelly.

Eight yards of printed linen. Eight pairs of kid mitts. Two pairs of silk shoes. A piece of flowered dimity. Two yards of fine cambric. Two caps. Two sets of ruffles. Two fans, two bonnets. A pair of silver sleeve buttons.

Of course, I was caught in the middle. I must side with Nelly when she complained to me about her grandmother.

I must promise Lady Washington I would keep an eye on her when I accompanied her to her social engagements.

The other girls accepted me, almost as an older sister. I was eighteen now.

"You're a Nigra?" Elizabeth Bordley asked our first day out in the carriage. "You don't look like one. I thought you were a cousin of Nelly's."

"She's closer to my grandmama than any cousin could be," Nelly said. "Aren't you, Oney?"

I did like their accepting me. And I acted as an older sister, reminding them not to wave at boys, not to appear without their neckerchiefs or gloves. I kept mindful of the time when we were to leave the homes of their friends.

But always I was careful. Once I delivered them inside and took their cloaks, I retreated to the kitchen, where the other servants gathered to talk.

It was on one of these occasions, in the kitchen of the Morris house, that I met Louise Sturgis, a free woman of color.

CHAPTER TWENTY
Winter 1791

She was young and slight, and her eyes were bright with merriment. Her neckerchief and apron were the whitest I'd ever seen, her hair wrapped in a blue turban. In the kitchen she served me coffee.

"So, you work for the Washingtons."

"Yes."

"You work for money? Or are you bound?"

I flushed. "I'm bound. But they're good to me. They treat me like a daughter."

"He gave money to our church. The first Negro church in America. So did Mr. Jefferson. Of course, it isn't built yet. We're planning on building it. That's the worst way to be, you know, treated like a daughter."

"Why?"

"It's another way of binding you to them."

I flushed again and gave the subject a turn. "A Negro church? I've never heard of one."

"Neither has anybody else. I've seen you driving around town with Nelly Custis in a fancy carriage. That little girl" — she shook her head and laughed — "in the bonnet with the peacock feather on it. They do get taken with vanity, these little white girls, don't they?"

I sat. "Yes, that's Nelly. But you should see her older sister Eliza."

"Don't want to. Nelly's enough for me. Looks like she can be a trial to her grandparents. Does he still plant tobacco?"

"What?"

She grinned, showing even white teeth. "Sorry, I have a way of jumping like a rabbit from one subject to another. My man says I always put the cart before the horse. Most Virginia planters are already in debt because the tobacco market is so bad. Does the president still plant tobacco?"

"No. He gave that up years ago. Says it wears out the land."

"He's a smart man. I've met a lot of Virginians here in Philadelphia. Here on a holiday. Most of them are still planting tobacco and can't make a profit anymore. Exports been falling off for thirty-five years already. Soon they all go bust. Their daughters are all frivolous. And their sons lazy and always with an eye for a pretty, young Negro wench. Their way of life is going to be over soon. Only thing is, they don't know it."

I was taken with her knowledge, her manner of speaking. She knew so much! I was also as confused as a mule in a mud hut. "What way of life?"

"Tobacco planting. Slavery."

My eyes went wide. "Slavery?"

She was kneading dough as we spoke. Her hands were quick and graceful. "You don't know? In 1780 they made a rule here in this city that all children born after that year will be free when they get to be twenty-eight. Massachusetts has no more slavery. Rhode Island and Connecticut have ruled for letting the slaves go free over the years. They call it emancipation."

"How do you know so much?"

"Any Negro, free or not, best make it their business these days to know. The laws change so fast. I was born free in New Jersey, though it was a slave state, my parents were free. But I was stolen and brought to a household here as a maid."

"Stolen?"

"Yes. Only, my mistress here was kind. She knew that slavery was wrong. So when my man came along and asked to buy me, she let me go. My man is Absalom Jones. He and Richard Allen are building the first Negro church. Dr. Benjamin Rush is helping them. You heard of Dr. Benjamin Rush?"

I felt so stupid, so lost. Just like the backwoods girl that I supposed I was. "Yes."

"He's a famous doctor here in Philadelphia. A friend of the president's. He signed the Declaration of Independence. Can you read and write?"

"I can read. And write some."

"What books do you read?"

Books? I didn't. I fell silent, embarrassed. "I don't," I admitted finally. "Don't think less of me. The general doesn't know I can read and write. Only Lady Washington does, and it's our secret."

She nodded. "I don't think less of you. What I think doesn't matter anyway. Most Negroes don't bother to read books, even if they can. Then they complain about their condition. It's their own fault. They don't even read the newspapers. You should at least do that. Keep up with what's going on, so you don't get caught unawares. And learn to think for yourself."

"I will," I promised. "And I do want to read, especially if it would make me as quick as you are about things."

"Next time you come, I'll have a book for you. Did you know that in the Philadelphia directory there are a hundred Negroes listed? Four are ministers and teachers, ten are artisans, and seventeen are tradespeople. I belong

194

to the Free African Society. It was started by Absalom and Richard Allen. We help Negroes to know what they are worth. And we are making a strong Negro community here in Philadelphia." She smiled, and her whole face was like a light in the darkest of nights. "Your Hercules belongs to our society."

"Hercules?"

"Yes. The president's dandy. He sells slops from the kitchen and struts about in those fancy clothes."

"Oh, no! Is he doing that here, too? He did that in New York!"

"He knows what he's about, girl, don't you fret. It's the way he came to our attention. We're helping him."

"Do what?" I did not have to ask. I knew.

"He wants to be free one day. We can do that for him. Or any other Negro who comes to us and asks." She looked at me slyly. She reminded me of somebody, but I could not think who.

"You keep your mouth shut about that, now. About everything I told you."

I left that day feeling as if I had been living underwater all my life, thrashing about, and I'd suddenly come up for air.

And when I finally did, I was struck by lightning.

I could not sleep that night, for thinking

of Louise. I kept hearing her voice, her perfect way of speaking. And I felt sad for all the Negroes I'd known on Mount Vernon.

I dreamed about her too. Only, in my dream, I heard Louise's voice, but the person standing in front of me was not Louise.

It was my mama. And I woke up crying because I knew then who Louise reminded me of. I lay in my bed staring out the window. There was a full moon. I missed the hooty owls back home.

She's what Mama would be like, I thought, *if Mama had the chance to be like anything. And that's why she's always put out with me. Because she knows her chance is gone. And I still have mine. And she wants me to take it.*

I kept a still tongue in my head about what I had learned. I was either blind or stupid, I decided. Right under my nose all kinds of things were going on with Negroes in Philadelphia.

What would Mama do if she heard about the Free African Society? What would Old Sinda have to say about the first Negro church?

It was all right here for me. And all I cared about was that I had a cozy room on the top floor.

Then came Louise, right next door in the

Morris house. Sometimes I'd see her out in the backyard, sweeping or putting some clothing out to air. If she saw me in the window, she'd wave.

One day when I looked out the window from my upstairs room, I saw she was alone in the yard. She saw me and beckoned I should come out, and ran back inside. I waited until she came out again, then downstairs and outside.

There was a wooden fence between the two yards. She came over to the fence and drew out a book from under her apron. "I didn't give it to you," she said.

I hid it under my apron and smuggled it upstairs, where I put it under the eaves.

That night I read it by a lone candle in my room. It was a primer, the kind used by young children. Another time when Nelly was visiting, Louise gave me *The Book of Common Prayer.*

Reading was like learning that I could breathe underwater, the same water I'd lived in all my life. There was a power to it that made me tremble.

I could do this! Just like white people!

The color of my skin did not stop me! And it was not reading recipes, either. It was strings of words that added up and made sense!

I felt smarter, quicker, and smug. Oh, so smug! No wonder white people walked around with their noses in the air all the time, acting superior.

It was reading that did it. Not being white. No wonder they kept us from doing it.

I hid the books under the eaves, where the slanted ceiling met the floor. I asked Louise for more. She gave them to me. I struggled through *Common Sense*, by Thomas Paine. The general had known Paine in the war. I labored through Phillis Wheatley's *Poems on Various Subjects, Religious and Moral*. Louise told me she was a Negro, a slave, and her work had been published in London less than twenty years ago!

I walked around in a daze, for months, the secret of my reading burning inside me.

February 1792

Christopher was bitten by a rabid dog.

I was in the kitchen when he came in that cold day. The dog had attacked him in the street. His hand was bleeding, and he was in great pain.

Lady Washington heard the commotion and came running. The general came from his study and immediately sent for a doctor and gave Christopher some brandy. But the doctor was not good with dog bites, he said.

198

He wrapped the hand. "There is a good man in Lebanon," he said. "A Dr. Stoy. If you value your servant, I would send him there. Dr. Stoy specializes in treating people bitten by mad animals."

That afternoon I helped Christopher pack his things. The general wrote him a letter, in the event that he was stopped on the road. "Show this to anyone who detains you," he said.

It had on it the signature of the president of the United States. George Washington.

Another letter gave him introduction to Dr. Stoy. The general also gave him twenty-five dollars. I walked to the backyard with Christopher.

"I wish Old Sinda was here," I said. "She'd make you a remedy and have you well."

"So do I." We stood for a moment, wrapped in the cold February wind, and the thought of Mount Vernon gave us both the miseries. "I'd give the hand to be back there now," Christopher said.

"Oh, Christopher."

"You miss it too?"

"Yes," I admitted.

"What's wrong with us? We're here in Philadelphia. The promised land for Negroes. The North. We can run anytime."

He met my eyes. I saw the question in his, but I had no answer for him. He mounted the horse the general was allowing him to take. "I got a horse, a pass from the general, and money," he said. "This is my chance, Oney." He looked down at me.

I reached up and took his good hand. "What will you do?"

"I got a strong feelin' to be free, Oney," he said. "I met lots of whites and free Negroes in this town already who would call me ten times a fool if I don't take it."

I nodded and watched him ride out of the yard. "Have a care, Christopher!" I called.

He waved without turning. I saw blood on the white sheeting around his hand. I knew I would never see him again. And I felt as bleeding and as bitten into as if the dog had attacked me.

CHAPTER TWENTY-ONE

It was determined by the general and Lady Washington that if Christopher mended, he would be back in three weeks.

Three weeks came and went, and there was no Christopher.

It was the end of March. One moment the skies over Philadelphia were blue with a warming sun, the next they were full of clouds and snowflakes. But the daffodils, the same as we had at Mount Vernon, which must have felt as stupid as I did in Philadelphia, stuck their heads above ground even in the snow.

"At home the asparagus will be growing," Lady Washington said sadly. "The strawberry vines and fruit trees will be showing their treasures. I miss home. Do you, Oney?"

I did, and it was no lie. We shared the feeling and it brought us closer.

But she did not speak of Christopher. Nobody spoke of Christopher. I expected never to see him again. I began to wonder where he had gone, who he had gone to. Austin scurried about doing Christopher's duties, but the general was not happy with Austin.

"My shaving water is cold!" I heard him yell in his bed chamber early one morning. And then there would be scurrying footsteps. *Nobody knows just the right moment to bring him his shaving water,* I thought. *Nobody but Christopher.*

In the kitchen the Negroes cast glances at one another, but no one said anything. And then on a day of chilling rain in the middle of April, I saw Christopher riding into the backyard.

And oh, I was glad! So glad to see him again! And oh, I was ashamed of my gladness.

I did not get the chance to speak to him until later that night. He was in the kitchen eating.

"Hey, Oney," he said.

"Hello, Christopher, how is the hand?"

"Healed." He showed me. I sat at the wooden table next to him, watching him eat. Waiting for him to speak.

Candles threw flickering light across our faces. "I couldn't do it, Oney," he said.

I nodded, waiting.

"That man's been good to me." He gestured in the direction of the main part of the house. "He saved my life, sending me to Lebanon. So I come back. With twelve dollars change. Hope you don't hate me for it, Oney."

"No, Christopher." I put my hand over his on the table. "I could never hate you."

If I did, I thought, *I am hating that part of you that I know is in myself.* We sat in silence, listening to the crackling of the fire in the hearth and the purring of the cat near it and the ticking of a nearby clock.

No, I thought. *I do not know if I could do it either.*

Summer 1792

Another summer, and we again went home.

"He's going to spirit his Negroes out of Philadelphia so you can't be emancipated," Louise said to me before we left.

"We're going home because we all miss it," I said.

We were in the kitchen of the Morris home again. "You know what, Louise? I *want* to go home," I said.

She was peeling apples for a pie. Just for a moment she stared at me, then dropped her gaze. "You disappoint me," she said.

"I know. But you don't know what it's like at Mount Vernon." I started to tell her, then her look stopped me. Anyway, I could never make her understand.

"You're defending your master," she said.

I was. I felt as if I had to protect the general when she said such things, and she said them more and more of late. "He's the president of the United States," I said.

She rolled her eyes.

I knew by now that there was some envy on the part of some Negroes I met in Philadelphia, because I was part of the household of President and Lady Washington. To me it was my everyday life. I'd known nothing else since I was a knee baby.

But I did not think Louise envious. She had too many other fish to fry. "No reason to defend his keeping slaves," she argued.

"I'm not defending his keeping slaves, I'm defending him," I told her. "And Lady Washington. They have been good to me. They are my family." I know how unseemly it sounded to her, but I meant it.

She hooted, sounding a lot like Mama. "Your family! Child, they're your family until they're ready to get rid of you. Then you're dirt to them."

"No," I insisted. "I'm more. I always have been. And Mount Vernon is home. You couldn't understand unless you lived there."

I had tears in my eyes.

"We're your community," she said. "At least we want to be. You are part of the Negro community whether you want to be or not, Oney Judge. The sooner you admit it, the better."

But I knew it already. I understood that I was part of Christopher, not wanting to leave. Wasn't I? And Louise's wanting me to leave? Did she think I didn't want it sometimes too?

But to her, my words sounded not like reasons, but excuses. She could do that to you, make you question everything you thought you held dear. She was like a housefly buzzing in your ear, causing a constant vexation.

But when we reached Virginia that year, I knew my words were true. Mount Vernon was home. I knew it when Nathan came out of the house to hug me. "Good to see you, Oney."

Nathan was like an older brother. And even with heat lying on the land like a damp blanket, with everything parched from drought, and not a leaf bestirring itself, I was glad to be there. The great white house enfolded us in its cooling elegance. I fell into its spell again.

It was a summer of drought, a summer of a middling Indian corn crop, a new well sunk opposite the greenhouse, of visits by Eliza to further plague me, of Mama laughing at me and saying cruel things because I was back again.

But it was a summer of new beginnings, and of endings, too.

Nathan had wed Esty, the seamstress who had taken Mama's place. She was pretty and accomplished and even helped him betimes in the kitchen. I was glad for the gift I had brought him, a new coverlet I had stitched for his bed. I made it a wedding present to them both.

But if that was a new beginning, the death of Old Sinda was an ending of things for us all. She had died from the flux shortly before we arrived.

Mount Vernon without Old Sinda! She'd been part and parcel of it since I'd first opened my eyes.

I went to the quarters to visit her cabin. In a minute I found myself surrounded by Negroes, all telling me what mischief Old Sinda had been up to since she died.

"We not wifout her," Lame Alice whispered to me. "She doan leave us alone. She alla time slip her skin and come out in de dark and torment us."

"She make de horses kick and yell in dere stalls at night," from another.

"She bother de chickens. De eggs too small," from a third.

I could feel Old Sinda's shadow lying over everything, not a cooling shadow, but like a lid on a pot of squash, keeping the heat under it.

Somehow they looked to me to do something about it. They looked up to me. I was dressed in printed muslin. I was Lady Washington's personal girl. I lived in Philadelphia. And I'd known Old Sinda since I was a child.

"I don't know how to conjure," I told them, "but I'll try to do something."

They stood back respectfully as I went into Old Sinda's cabin. It was empty, hot and dusty. I saw her remedies in stone jars on a shelf, her bowl and pestle, her narrow bed. I closed my eyes, trying to summon her spirit, but she would not be summoned.

When I opened them again, I spied the conch shell on the shelf next to the jars. And I remembered how, when I was a child, she'd told me she'd brought it with her when she came on the slave ship from Africa.

"Water bring us here, water take us home," she'd said. I held the brittle old shell in my hands. Was it really from far across the sea in Africa? I tried to remember the tribal names Sambo Anderson had taught me as a child.

Whydahs, Asante, Fanti, Ibo, Coromantees, I thought. *Ga, Hausa. Gone. All gone. Old, beautiful Africa puke up its own and sell them for slaves.*

"Is this what you want, Sinda?" I asked. And the sound of my own voice in the empty cabin startled me. "You want the conch shell to take you back across the water? To take you home?"

But I knew it was what she wanted. And I knew then what I must do.

On the way out I also picked up her bowl and pestle. Then I called several Negro children to me, and together we walked down the path to the slave cemetery. The older folk followed. Even Nathan and Esty.

I had the Negro children walk across Old Sinda's grave to quiet her spirit so she wouldn't slip her skin and trouble them anymore.

I put the conch shell and the bowl and pestle on her grave. They bore part of her spirit. She might need them, especially the conch shell. "The water brought you here, Sinda," I said. "The water will take you home."

Behind me the old slaves were singing softly. Then I took some of the dust from her grave and put it in a small sack to take back to Philadelphia.

Old Sinda was part of the Gone.

"You did good, Oney," Nathan told me. "I'm glad you didn't forget the old ways."

The Negroes were still singing when Nathan, Esty, and I went back to the house.

The next day the Negroes from the quarters told me the children had had a peaceful night. But there was another spirit haunting Mount Vernon that only I knew about.

Louise was here with me.

It wasn't that housefly buzzing in my ear. It was Louise being a vexation every time I languished in some sweet happening.

"Sure, you look pretty in your soft yellow muslin, but look out there at those hoe Negroes," I knew she would say, "never ceasing their sowing and grubbing and trimming."

And when I walked on the piazza with Lady Washington: "Look at them out in that hot sun thrashing the buckwheat. Look at how sick Bosun and Charlotte are with the flux. Your master feels guilty, that's why he sends for Dr. Craik."

Dr. Craik ordered rice water mixed with honey for Bosun and Charlotte.

Before I left I told Nathan about Louise. I swore him to secrecy. "I doan know how Northern Negroes are, Oney," he said. "But I would suppose they be different from us.

All I can say is, you do what you think is best when the time comes. But be sure it's what you want. That's all that matters."

When we left, I hugged him for dear life. Nathan, my brother, who had taught me to read and write, who had taught me just about everything.

January 1793

"Oney Judge, you're so slow! You got molasses in your veins instead of blood, I swear. If you don't hurry, we'll miss that balloon!"

"We do not swear, Eliza," Lady Washington scolded. But it was only a mild scolding, as always.

I came running from the kitchen with two hot bricks wrapped in flannel, for Eliza's feet. Her feet were always cold, and we were going in the general's carriage to see the aeronaut Jean Pierre Blanchard, who was to take off in his balloon.

"He'll fall on our heads," Patsy worried.

"He'll blow across the river first," the general said. "And fall on his own head." He was always ready to joke with his grandchildren.

"I'd like to be going up there with him. Could I someday, Grandpapa?" Wash asked.

The general helped his wife and grandchildren into the carriage. I set the bricks at

Eliza's feet. "Attend to your studies first, young man," the general said. "And who knows who will be flying in what when you come into a man's estate."

We had a place of honor, of course, around Independence Hall that cold day. "Couldn't he do this in summertime?" Eliza complained.

"If he did, you'd be complaining about the heat," Nelly told her.

We watched as the great balloon rose in the air and drifted overhead in the blue sky. People oohed and aahed, clapped and whistled.

And I wished my mama and Nathan and Esty and others I loved at Mount Vernon could have a balloon too. To fly here to Philadelphia.

It was only proper, being that Nelly visited so often at the Morris house, that Maria come to ours. And so Louise came with her. I trembled when we sat in the kitchen and it was my turn to act as hostess to her. I urged her, in whispers, not to speak out about her doings in the free Negro community of Philadelphia.

And so she kept a still tongue in her head in the general's kitchen. But I was starting to feel that she expected something from me.

211

What did she expect? That I would one day appear at the Morrises' kitchen with my things stuffed in a pillowcase and say I was running away? She was becoming more and more a vexation to me. She made my vitals hurt. Her mind never stayed still. She was always moving on to the next task. And she could not abide my staying still. She had no patience with a Negro who was satisfied with her lot.

What she expected from me now, I soon discovered, was my attending a meeting of the Free African Society.

I made excuses all that winter. Then finally one spring afternoon I decided to go just to end her nagging. Lady Washington gave me Wednesday afternoons off. The meeting was held in the cellar of one member's home. I brought some sewing because that was what we were supposed to be doing. Sewing and having tea.

They didn't shilly-shally, but got right to the matter at hand. "You want to be free," Louise whispered. "We can see to it that you become free."

There were six of them, all women, the youngest sixteen, the oldest with short, graying hair. Their hands kept busy, knitting and sewing for poor people in their community.

"I will be free someday," I told them.

Some of them admired my dress. It was made of India Jaquinett muslin. Phoebe, the sixteen-year-old, touched the fabric. "Where did you get it?"

I blushed. "Mr. Jefferson brought it home from Paris. He gave it to Lady Washington, and she allowed me some."

They would think I was taken with vanity, using Mr. Jefferson's name. Phoebe sniffed. "No wonder you don't wish to be free," she said.

"Hush, Phoebe. This hasn't got to do with dresses," Louise scolded. "Oney knows dresses are no account. Don't you, Oney?"

"Yes," I answered quietly.

She leaned across the table. "He signed the Fugitive Slave Act, your master. You know what that means?"

I knew she was going to bring that up. Inside I groaned.

"It means," she said, "that slave owners can cross state lines to get back their runaways. And your President Washington signed it."

There was silence in the kitchen. Nobody said anything.

Louise went on. "We know a ship captain, name of John Bowles. From Portsmouth, New Hampshire. He runs harnesses, bridles, saddles, and other leather goods out of Philadelphia to Portsmouth on the *Nancy* a few times a year. And betimes he takes a Negro from Philadelphia to Portsmouth too. It's safe up there for runaways."

I was taken aback. "You mean, if I leave, I have to go farther north?"

"Course you would, child." Louise laughed. "You couldn't stay here! Not in Philadelphia! A runaway from the president's house? They'd scour the city for you! Didn't you tell me what the president thinks of Negroes who run away?"

"A betrayal," I said. "He cannot forgive betrayal."

The whole thing was too terrible to study on.

But not for Louise. She wanted nothing else but to think on it. "Why do you think Christopher didn't take his freedom?" she asked me. "Where would he get work? The one thing that will recommend him, he can't talk about. He worked for the president of the United States. You think anybody's going to want him? The runaway servant of the president of the United States?"

"Then why would they want me?" I asked.

"Because we're helping you. We know people who would want you, who would want to help you. If Christopher had come to us, we could have helped him."

"I'll be free someday," I said again. "In a way that I won't have to run. Old Sinda back home told me."

She laughed. Just like Mama. "An old saltwater Negro who was half crazy and practiced voodoo," she said. "Girl, you gotta forget back home. You gotta forget about the Washingtons being your family. He signed the Fugitive Slave Act. Didn't you hear me?"

"He had to," I shot back. "As president, he has to keep the whole country happy. Not just the abolitionists in the North."

"Well!" And she put her hand on her hip, sassy like. "Aren't we smart these days?"

"You told me to read the newspapers," I said. "I've been reading them."

"Yeah, well, you just remember. We are your only chance."

CHAPTER TWENTY-TWO

When word had come to the general about the execution of Louis XVI, he was very upset.

"France is now a republic," I heard him tell Lady Washington, "and they will want us to recognize them as a republic. And they will want us to repay the debts we owe them from our revolution."

Wash and Nelly were taken with the idea of people getting their heads cut off. I heard Wash telling a friend about the guillotine one day. So did the general. And he scolded Wash.

"We do not take delight in the misfortunes of others," he said.

Another thing that happened that spring is that the household acquired two pets. A parrot named Snipe and a dog named Frisk.

The children were delighted, of course. Frisk was small, brown and white, and fuzzy, unlike the hounds the general kept at home for hunting. Moreover, Frisk stayed in the house, in the manner of dogs in other quality Philadelphia families. Frisk slept with Wash, in his bed.

The parrot had its own cage in the back parlor, and the parrot talked. Of course, one of the first things Wash taught it to say was, "Off with their heads, off with their heads." And when guests came, it was my job to cover Snipe's cage so his embarrassing squawks would not be heard, because when you covered his cage, he thought it was night and kept silent.

Still another thing that happened is that the general was elected for a second term as president.

Lady Washington was not happy. "Four more years of this?" she said to me as she wrote home to Mount Vernon to have some shad sent. "Mr. Jefferson says North and South will hang together if they have my husband to hang with. Humph. How much is he supposed to give?"

I must ask Louise why the North and South would want to separate. She knew the answers to all sorts of things like that. And despite the vexation she caused me, I found that I now wanted to know too.

I was sick in my heart from the disagreement with Louise. For weeks we did not see each other. If I went with Nelly to the Morris house, she made it her business not to be there.

I could see, more and more, that she was like my mama. She knew she held sway over me. She wanted me to agree with everything she said.

No, she wanted me to think for myself. But not if it differed with her way of thinking.

"Ice cream, Oney! We must have ice cream!" Eliza fair screamed it as we alighted from the carriage on Walnut Street.

Eliza and Patsy were visiting again. Together, with Nelly, we were going to the theater.

Patsy was betrothed, and her not yet seventeen! Her young man, from Georgetown, was Thomas Peter, whose father was a judge and a friend of the general's.

"I love ice cream!" Patsy cried. "And the theater! Oh, aren't we fortunate to be here in Philadelphia in the spring?"

"You are," Eliza said snidely. Eliza was seventeen, with no betrothal in sight. And she made no secret of her envy for her younger sister. Nelly, at fourteen, was nothing but admiring of her older sisters, whatever they did.

"You'd best get your fill of ice cream and theater this day, Patsy," Eliza said. "Once you're married and a matron, you'll do nothing but bear children and become mistress of your needle."

"Stop it, you two," I scolded. "Your grandma told you not to plague your sister that way, Eliza. So hush!"

She nudged me as we walked along the cobblestone walk to the theater door. "Posh!" she said. "You can't scold me, Oney Judge. We grew up together."

"I'm the oldest," I reminded her. "And sent along to keep you all acting proper."

"And so?" Eliza pouted. "If I kissed a boy, would you tell Grandmama?"

"There are no boys hereabouts to kiss," I said.

"I'd tell," Nelly said.

"You!" Eliza pinched her. "You think you're Grandmama's favorite just because you live with her. And Wash is spoiled worse than our daddy ever was."

But it was all in good fun, the teasing. It was spring. Shadows of newly budding tree limbs danced on the sidewalk. Vendors sold bunches of flowers on the street, as well as roasted corn. The girls were dressed in pastel silks that made them look like tulips. I wore a new printed muslin. And as we walked on the cobblestone sidewalk men who recognized them as President Washington's granddaughters tipped their hats. We preened and giggled and exchanged secrets, just like girls everywhere have been doing in springtime from the beginning of time.

And if the men who tipped their hats for us that day thought that I, near white, was one of the general's granddaughters too, was that my fault?

It was all in good fun, wasn't it?

We went to the theater four times that spring. We saw Shakespeare's plays, and Patsy had tears running down her face, no doubt being caught in the throes of romantic love. We went for ice cream afterward at a new type of establishment called an ice cream parlor. We went to the circus, where they had a real elephant, and to Peale's Museum and the Philadelphia waxworks.

We went to concerts, to the park.

Always I had a new dress, a leghorn hat to keep the sun from my face. Always I was given the money by Lady Washington to pay. Because I was the oldest, they looked up to me, asked my advice about things, even asked for stories about their grandma and grandpa.

I told them how the general's mama had been struck by lightning while he was in her womb. How Lady Washington's father had taken in a Negro boy and raised him as his own.

They knew I was closer to their grandma than even they were most of the time. They knew that I could curry favor with her for them if they had an unusual request.

I was an older sister to them. And I loved the role.

And then, one day, it happened.

We'd just come home from a lecture in the bottom room of an Episcopal church, Eliza and I. The lecture was on the French Revolution.

Eliza had begged to go, saying it was part of her education, wasn't it? I had interceded for her with Lady Washington, as I had on some other occasions, and Eliza was filled with a whole host of new good feelings about me.

So tea was spread for us and Lady Washington in the parlor. "It's so good to see you girls all enjoying yourselves," Lady Washington said. "And Oney, I can't help notice how you and Eliza are getting on these days."

We both beamed. It was true. But when

girls have a secret together, they do get on, don't they?

Eliza and I had a secret.

It was the real reason she was attending the lectures. She didn't give a fig for the revolution in France. She didn't care how many people got their heads chopped off.

There was a man at the lectures, however, who'd already given her the eye. An Englishman named Thomas Law. He appeared to be a man of wealth, and Eliza was quite taken with him.

In a few words at tea after the lecture he was introduced to her. And told her he lived in a very elegant and great house on New Jersey Avenue in the new federal city.

I did not like him. He'd been to India and had been married. His boys were near as old as Eliza, three of them.

"He's an old man," I told Eliza on the way home.

"He's thirty-nine," she shot back. "And he's going to call on me here. Don't tell Grandmama and Grandpapa about his previous marriage. Not just yet. Please, Oney?"

So I kept a still tongue in my head. I knew it was wrong. But Eliza was desperate about being wed. The fact that her younger sister was marrying before her undid her completely.

And so I earned her trust, her niceness. And spineless creature that I was, it was important to me.

I was not true to myself. And so I sealed my own fate.

"You know, with this young man coming to call on you," Lady Washington said, "we ought to give some thought, Eliza, to your future. I am giving Patsy two of my dower Negroes for her wedding. Since you and Oney get on so well, how about we think of my giving Oney to you when you wed? Would you like that?"

I felt a thunderclap in my head.

My hands went cold. A sweat broke out on my forehead.

My hands were shaking so, I had to set down my teacup.

Eliza shrieked and leaped up to kiss her grandma. "He's only coming to call, Grandmama. I'm not going to wed yet, though I secretly feel as if our fates are linked already. Isn't that wonderful, Oney?" She turned to me. "Grandmama is going to give you to me as one of my wedding presents! Just like she's giving Patsy two of her dower Negroes, she's giving you to me. You're a dower Negro too. At least your mama was. You know that, don't you, Oney?"

She said it as if I should be proud. For the

moment I did not understand the true meaning of it, however.

"We'll be together!" She was jumping up and down. "And that's how it should be, Oney, because you were with me when I met Thomas. Oh, I'm so happy."

She grabbed my hands in her own. "Oney, you are my lucky charm. Grandmama's gift of you to me will bring about my betrothal, I just know it! But why are your hands so cold? Grandmama, her hands are freezing! Give her some brandy. I must keep her well. She is going to be mine!"

At Mount Vernon there was a swampy ravine that was so misty and damp it was a breeding place for mosquitoes. And mosquitoes carried malaria.

The general had named that place the Hell Hole.

For the week following Lady Washington's announcement to me I felt like I was living in the middle of the Hell Hole. I felt strangled by mists. My brain could not clear itself free.

I kept telling myself what happened had not happened. That I had not heard it.

Then in the next moment I knew I had. And it made sense.

I was the daughter of one of Lady Washington's dower slaves, the Negroes she had brought to Mount Vernon with her when she wed.

As such, I belonged to her, not the general.

He could free all his slaves upon his death if he wished. But I was her slave. I had been laboring under a false sense of security for years now.

Why had this thought never come to me?

Mama had been right all these years. So was Louise.

The general could free all his slaves upon his death. But I would not be one of them.

Thomas Law did come to call on Eliza, three times when she was staying in Philadelphia. Then he returned to the federal city. And Eliza went home to Virginia.

"He's promised to come call on me there, Oney," she said.

She was smitten with him.

I knew what I must do, though I was ashamed to do it.

I must do it soon. Or I'd end up in the new federal city that was being built, with Thomas and Eliza. In slavery for the rest of my life.

I must go to Louise for help.

"How could Lady Washington do this to me, Louise?"

We were in the kitchen of the Morris house. She sat next to me at the table. "She didn't do anything to you, child. You did it to yourself."

I wiped away my tears and listened.

Her voice was kind but knowing. "I kept telling you. So did your mama, from what I hear. You did it to yourself, believing that her goodness was love. It wasn't. She's just a good lady. But you're a Negro, not her child. And she's just acting like a mistress does with her Negroes."

I told her then about the general's will. "But I'm a dower slave," I said. "I belong to her, not him."

"That's right. Now you're starting to understand."

"Louise, I won't be given to Eliza. I hate the man she's courting. He's no good for her. I won't be in servitude to him. And once she weds, Eliza will go back to being bossy with me like she was before. And I won't be given to somebody for a wedding present. Like a horse or a parcel of land."

She leaned toward me. She brushed my hair off my face. "Then, you know what you have to do, Oney Judge, don't you?"

"Yes," I sobbed.

"Quiet, now. Best this happened, we can plan. And we gotta plan," she said.

"How?"

"You have to save money, Oney, for when you run. You can't just run without a shilling in your pocket. Why do you think Hercules has been selling his slops from the kitchen? You have to sew some strong, warm clothes. It's cold up in New Hampshire. I have to make contacts. It could take time."

"How long?" I asked worriedly.

"A year," she said. "Maybe longer. But we'll help you, child. Don't you worry."

"Suppose Eliza weds before then?"

"I misdoubt she will. They're just planning Patsy's marriage for next year. Eliza won't wed before that. And if we get a whiff that she will, we'll spirit you away, don't worry. But we're going to make every effort to do this right for you."

And so we planned. I would stitch aprons, caps, even dresses, and Louise would sell them for me. Lady Washington approved of my sewing in my free moments. And I would make a quantity of warm clothing for myself, in secret.

All that spring I stayed awake half the night sewing. I hoarded the money from the garments Louise sold, and envied Hercules.

For he had known from the first what he must do. And he was willing to play the fool to do it.

That summer letters came from Mount Vernon. My aunt Myrtilla and Sambo Anderson had died. So had George Augustine, who had been running the plantation.

I felt the ending of things. I felt as if God was taking them so I would have no more ties at Mount Vernon. Sambo Anderson and Aunt Myrtilla. The general and Lady Washington mourned George Augustine, and the general took a short trip home to see him properly buried.

And then that summer something happened that nobody could do anything about, Negro or white. And it caused deep concern to us all.

Yellow fever came to Philadelphia.

CHAPTER TWENTY-THREE

The first we knew of it was when Wash's school was closed in June because so many children were complaining of fever.

That summer the city was hotter than inside the devil's ear. The heat had started in late May. Ice was brought to the general's house twice a day.

By June we heard of the death of an unfortunate woman who had made a living selling oysters in a cellar on Front Street.

"They say she went out of her senses, Grandmama," Wash said one evening at dinner. "Her name was Clarey."

"And I heard today," Nelly put forth, "that five people died in one house on Chestnut Street. They had malignant fevers."

"Well, you shan't go to school, then," Lady Washington told them. "General, we mustn't send them."

He agreed. "I'm concerned about Alexander Hamilton," he said. "In a cabinet meeting yesterday he complained of a head-ache."

We soon found out that Alexander Hamilton, a favorite of the general's who was secretary of the treasury, had yellow fever. The general sent around Dr. Rush, who was already tending many patients.

More and more people fell sick every day as the summer came about with full force.

Lady Washington kept us inside. She had the house servants sprinkle sulfur about and wash everything down with vinegar. She would not allow guests. Or tutors, and of course that made both young people happy.

By the end of June we heard that Dr. Hutchinson, another noted physician, was dead.

People started leaving the city. When you looked out the windows, all you saw were wagons loaded with household goods and servants walking beside them. Barrels of tar were set afire on every street corner, in spite of the heat, to ward off the pestilence. And the smell of the tar assaulted the senses.

Children wandered, uncared for, on the streets. And it was soon discovered that the grown-ups inside their houses had all died. Dead people lay in the ditches where they dropped, until the dead cart came to take them away.

It came in the evening. As the oil lamps were lit you would hear the clop-clop-clopping of the horse's hooves and the doleful cry of the driver. "Bring out your dead! Bring out your dead!"

In the middle of the night I heard the cry, and when I looked out the open window into the soft summer night, I saw the terrible shadow of the dead cart, larger than life, on the front of the house across the street. I saw people dragging a body out a door. I heard the wailing.

Wild dogs wandered the streets, nipping at the fingers of the dead. Pigs rooted among them.

Lady Washington wouldn't allow her servants out either. Congress shut down. The president's cabinet did not meet. Schools closed. Merchants refused to sell to people. Ships refused to drop anchor in the port once word went out to sea about yellow fever in Philadelphia. People stopped attending church, and those who did said the ministers were telling them that the fever was God's punishment on the people of Philadelphia for their wantonness and sins. That they should shut down their saloons and theaters and concert halls. Their gambling halls and racetracks.

They were already shut down. Nobody

was going anywhere. Servants who managed to slip out and bring home some tea or fruit from a ship whose captain did dare drop anchor talked about black vomit and bloody bile.

The hot midday streets were deserted.

"We ought to leave," the general told Lady Washington. "We should get the children out of the city. We should go home."

"I'll not leave," Lady Washington said, "until September, when it is time to go home. And if you, the president, leave, people will say you are abandoning them. You will incite criticism."

So we stayed. The general continued to worry about Alexander Hamilton. Thomas Jefferson sent a note around: "Last week there were eighty deaths in the city. I fear that this week there will be two hundred."

The days dragged. The windows and curtains of the house were closed to keep out the midday sun. I missed the fresh air, but if you opened a window or door, all you smelled was tar burning in the barrel in the middle of the backyard.

The clocks ticked in agonizing slowness as the children tried to read and keep busy. The Negro servants, frightened out of their wits, slipped about, their shadows larger than life on the walls.

"Bring out your dead! Bring out your dead!" It was Snipe's latest bit of sassiness. That parrot always knew to say the worst things. I think Wash taught him. And the general was getting ready to give him to a ship's master on the wharves.

Food in the house was running low. Christopher and Austin, allowed out only to walk Frisk, were given permission to go out at night to the wharves, because we'd heard a ship from the South had dropped anchor with a cargo of fresh fruit, rice, and other necessities. When they came back with the bounty, the general made them strip and wash down out in the yard. And all the clothing they'd worn was burned.

These were the instructions to the general from Dr. Rush.

Then, in August, a note came around from Dr. Rush. The general assembled us all in the back parlor and read it to us.

" 'My dear Mr. President: I will not leave the city as long as I can still treat its people. But I have had recent reports that Africans are immune to the yellow fever. We are desperately in need of help. I have been in touch with Negro ministers, and my friend Richard Allen is going to ask Negro citizens to serve as aides to the doctors, gravediggers, and drivers of the dead carts. If this be true, that they are immune, I think we are twice blessed. They can help us in this terrible struggle and gain respect from the white population for doing so. I can promise them that their efforts will be well rewarded. If you want to volunteer any of your Negro servants, I would be most gratified.' "

Christopher, of course, wanted to go. So did Austin and Paris. I offered. I had heard from Nelly that Louise Sturgis was going. The Morrises had allowed it, as long as she did not come back at night, until the nightmare was over.

If she lived through it and came back at all.

But the general said no. Nobody could assure him that his servants were immune. And he would not allow us to go.

The Negroes who did go could be seen on the streets, picking up the dead, driving the dead carts, delivering food to sick houses. And burying the dead in Potter's Field outside town. In the Dutch Calvinist Church grounds and in the Friends Meetinghouse graveyard.

In August the general moved us to a modest fieldstone house in Germantown, eight miles outside the city. Before the pestilence passed, six thousand people in Philadelphia died.

We waited out the summer in the country. On September 10 we were supposed to leave again for Mount Vernon.

I forgot about running away. I slacked off from my sewing. I'd fallen again under the spell of the general and Lady Washington. Then, the day before we were supposed to leave, Christopher smuggled a note to me.

"It's from Absalom Jones," he said. "A peddler brought it by."

Absalom wrote that Louise Sturgis was well, though she had fallen ill with the fever. She looked forward to seeing me again in late fall. And I should keep up with my sewing. We had much to talk about.

My heart fell. The yellow fever had spared us, and I knew I should be thankful. But now that it was over, I had to face my problems again, and I did not want to.

We went home again to Mount Vernon.

I had a moment's misgiving about going. Would I be placing myself in danger? I wouldn't be in the free North. And since I now knew what Lady Washington planned for me, I worried. But then, Eliza wouldn't wed for another year. I'd be safe until then, I was sure of it. Besides, though some servants stayed in Philadelphia, it was still deserted from the fever. The Washingtons would never let me go back there.

So I went home again.

The general was not happy. At Dogue Run only half the wheat was in. The clover was ready to be cut, but the machine to cut it with couldn't be found. William Pearce of Maryland, who was well recommended, came to Mount Vernon for an interview to replace George Augustine.

He had a wife and children. He would live in the mansion house, above and below the banquet hall. I hoped the general would hire him, and he did, for one year in which he would prove himself. At one hundred guineas, with pork and beef provisions and bread, the use of three cows and three slaves, the permission to raise his own poultry, full power over all the overseers on the other farms, and fodder for his horses.

I was glad. The place would be well cared for. I worried about it as if it were my own. And that worried me more than anything.

For I knew that one of these years I would not be back again.

I visited everyone, saying good-bye until the next visit.

Mama hugged me tight, then pushed me back, holding on to my shoulders. "You go soon," she said.

I nodded, scarce able to speak. Neither one of us could speak of it now that the time was coming near. But being a mama, she knew I'd go, soon as I could.

Nathan and Esty were expecting their first child. "I will rock her to sleep when I next come," I said.

But when I looked into Nathan's eyes, I saw he knew too. I was lying. Nathan knew me. He knew that if I had my own way, I'd never be home again.

CHAPTER TWENTY-FOUR
Spring–Summer 1795

They were going to cut off the head of the wife of the Marquis. That was the talk all through the general's house in Philadelphia that spring and summer.

"Her name is Adrianne," Nelly told me.

It was all Nelly talked about. At sixteen, she was taken with the romance of it. "But my grandpapa worked in secret, with Thomas Jefferson, to keep her head from being cut off."

We were out for a Saturday-afternoon springtime walk. "She was spared," Nelly went breathlessly, "at the foot of the guillotine. My grandpapa intervened for her, through Mr. Jefferson. And now her son comes to Boston! Oh, I heard he is sad eyed and lonely. And just my age. I begged Grandpapa to bring him here. But he said no, he can't; it has something to do with silly old politics. He can't welcome the son of Lafayette, because he mustn't take sides in the war between France and England. I hate politics, Oney."

"I do too," I said. "But for another reason."

"What? Tell me?"

"Well . . ." I hesitated, then spoke. "Don't tell your grandpa."

"Of course I won't. You can trust me."

I knew I could. "Your grandpa signed the Fugitive Slave Act two years ago."

"Oh, that." Nelly waved a hand. "It has naught to do with you. All it means is that if a slave runs away, the master can cross state lines to get him back." She sighed. "I had to learn about it in school. So dreadful boring. You know Grandpapa had to do it. He can't go against our neighbors at home in Virginia. He wants to go back home for good someday."

"I know," I said.

"Oney. Don't worry it so. You'll not be running off." She giggled. "And if you did, I just can't imagine Grandpapa chasing after you."

We laughed, as girls do. Then the talk returned to the young Lafayette again. "His name is George Washington de Lafayette," she whispered. "His daddy was in prison for five years."

"I remember him," I said.

"Do you?"

"Yes," I told her. "I remember how he visited at Mount Vernon, and some things he said."

"What?" Nelly pushed. "What did he say?"

"Oh, nothing. I remember the way he talked. With that French accent."

"Oh," Nelly said, "I do wish Grandpapa would let his son come here!"

February 1796

"Eliza is getting married, Louise," I said. "She told the Washingtons yesterday. She wants to marry this year."

We sat on a bench in the warm sun of a February afternoon. We sat staring at the new Negro church at Sixth and Lombard Streets, within the shadow of Independence Hall. Richard Allen, friend of Louise's Absalom, had built the church out of a blacksmith shop. Allen had had horses drag the blacksmith shop to the empty lot several weeks before. Now it had a peaked roof and a cross, proper windows, and pews inside.

"What is Mr. Allen going to call his church?" I asked.

"Bethel. In Hebrew it means 'house of God.' That Eliza is a fine-looking girl. Why is she throwing herself away on a man twice her age, with three grown sons?"

"She's smitten with him."

"Is the general going to allow it?"

"All he asks is that Mr. Law doesn't take her back to England. That he keep her in this country."

"Well" — Louise took my hand — "you know what you have to do, then, if they're going to wed this year. How much money do you have saved?"

"I have near a hundred dollars."

"You know your worth on the auction block?"

I blushed. "No."

"I'd say about two hundred, being that you were taught to be a private ladies' maid. If you had a child, you'd both go for three hundred. You want me to make contact with Captain Bowles?"

I didn't answer for a moment, then I did. "I won't go with Eliza when she weds, Louise. I've met Mr. Law. It's more than just leaving Mount Vernon and the Washingtons. I don't like the way Mr. Law looks at me. And I'll be his slave. Forever."

She nodded slowly, knowing. "Captain Bowles makes the trip from Portsmouth to Philadelphia once a month. Our people can arrange to have you slipped aboard. When do they go again to Mount Vernon?"

"In June. I heard the general telling his secretary. In June, Louise! This is his last year as president. I know he will serve until the end of the year, but I'm afraid that if I go to Mount Vernon in June, Lady Washington will turn me over to Eliza down there and I'll never come back to Philadelphia. I feel it in my bones."

"So, we must act, then. You should leave before June."

"Yes," I said.

"Captain Bowles has taken our people in the past, Oney. But always they slip aboard when his back is turned. And with you we must be especially careful. He must not know who you are. He must not know that you are the favored slave of the wife of the president of the United States. Even if you speak to him on the voyage, you must not tell him."

The voyage! The word made it all real somehow. "Yes," I said.

Sometimes when I was out walking in Philadelphia that spring, I would look around and think: *I won't ever be coming back here again. And it is part of my life. What will I do when I can no longer walk these streets?*

And then I would think: *But what will I do when I can no longer see Mount Vernon again? When the elegant white house reaches out its arms to enfold me and I am not there? No more will I hear the peepers in the coves of the river, see the mist hanging over it in the evenings, look out over the bowling green and feel cared for and loved.*

I will never see Nathan and Esty's little girl! What will Nathan say when he's heard I've run? I will never see my mama again. Or Lame Alice or the deer in the paddock or old Nelson, the general's horse.

Can I do this? Where will I end? What will be my fate? A cold room alone in a boardinghouse in Portsmouth, New Hampshire?

And my heart would like to burst, thinking on it.

Then I would think: *But what happens if I don't do it? I won't live anymore at Mount Vernon anyway. I'll never come back to Philadelphia anyway. Eliza and Mr. Law are going to live in the new federal city. And mayhap he won't keep his promise to the general. Mayhap he'll take her to England.*

But my heart would like to burst anyway.

And then I would think: *Why can't the general save me, like he saved the Marquis's wife? Why can't I ask him? I've known him all my life.*

But I knew. Because I was not an aristocrat about to have her head cut off. I was only a dower slave girl who belonged to his wife. And she could do with me as she pleased.

CHAPTER TWENTY-FIVE
April 1796

"Christopher, I'm leaving."

"This time of night? You want me to walk you to wherever you're goin', Oney?"

"No." I took his arm and led him out from under the window of the kitchen. The April air was balmy. In the distance I heard the music from the spinet inside the house. Nelly was playing. Candlelight glowed in the windows.

"Christopher," I said. "I'll be leaving soon. I wanted you to be one to know."

It was dusk, but not too dim for me to see the understanding light in his eyes. "Oney, you doan mean it."

"Yes. I do. I just wanted to tell you, Christopher. Don't talk me out of it. I must go. I must be strong and go. If I don't, Lady Washington is going to give me to Eliza and Mr. Law when they wed."

He scowled. "Where you goin'?"

"I can't say, Christopher." I could, but I

wouldn't. When he was questioned by the general, I wanted him to be able to say, in truth, that he did not know where I had gone. Or how. Oh, it tore at my vitals, having to have this conversation with Christopher. It did!

He nodded. "When?" he asked.

"Soon. That's all I know. I won't be going back to Mount Vernon with them in June. I'll miss you, Christopher," I said. "And everyone."

Tears were gathering in the corners of his eyes. "Anythin' I can do for you, Oney?"

"Yes. When you go back in June, you can pet the deer in the paddock for me. You can hold Nathan and Esty's baby. Give old Nelson some sugar. You can" — I drew in my breath and let it out slowly — "tell my mama she was right. And I love her."

"You sure 'bout what you're doin', Oney?"

"I was never so sure of anything in my life, Christopher. But that doesn't mean it doesn't hurt me. Being sure doesn't make it hurt any less, Christopher. That's all."

"Girl, you doin' the right thing. An' I'll be followin' soon after you go," Hercules said.

It was late at night. We were in the

kitchen. Outside on the street the town crier went by, giving the hour. Ten of the clock and all was well.

I was in my long nightgown. I'd crept down because I knew Hercules would be in the kitchen alone at this hour.

"You, Hercules?" I asked. "When?"

"After this trip to Mount Vernon. This be my last. I gots to tell my little daughter there goodbye."

"Hercules, the general will not be able to abide not having you for a cook," I said.

"I knows that. Just like I knows Lady Washington gonna cry when you go."

"Oh, Hercules — don't, please."

"That woman love you, Oney."

"Then, why is she giving me to Eliza?"

"She gettin' old. So is the general. I guess she just wanna keep you in the family. See you sometimes."

"Like a pet?" I asked.

He said nothing for a moment. "Like a member of the family," he said.

"You aren't being fair, Hercules. I have to go, just like you do."

He was chopping vegetables, setting them aside for a dish he would make tomorrow. "I know what I gots to do, Oney Judge," he said. "And I know what you gots to do. And you are right. Same as I am right. But I still say, like a member of the family. That's all I say, Oney Judge, that's all."

May 1796

The general was dictating a letter to his secretary, Bartholomew Dandridge. The letter was to William Pearce, who was now managing Mount Vernon.

Outside the door of the general's study, I listened.

"Let the house in the upper garden, called the schoolhouse, be cleaned and got in order against my return. Glass put in the windows if wanted, and a lock on the door. I cannot yet say with certainty when I shall be able to visit Mount Vernon but hope it will be by, or before, the middle of June. Have good meats ready for us by that time; and tell the gardener I shall expect an abundance of everything in the gardens, and to see everything in prime order there."

I ran upstairs to get my things, which were tied in a bundle.

Tonight, after everyone in the house was asleep, I would slip out. A block from the general's house Louise would be waiting. I would give her the bundle. In it would be not only my clothing, but my books. And my small bag of goofer dust from Old Sinda's grave. Louise would keep the bundle until such time as the *Nancy* dropped anchor at the docks for its May visit to Philadelphia.

The warm air of the May evening drifted in the open windows of the dining room of the president's house as he and Lady Washington sat at supper.

Nelly was at the table with them. Wash was off to college in Princeton, New Jersey. "I'll miss the friends I made here," Nelly was saying.

"You can invite them to Mount Vernon when I retire," the general told her.

"I've spent eight years here," Nelly said wistfully. "I've learned French, Italian, and Spanish. I've been to the theater and to the best schools. But I'll be glad to be going home at the end of the year, Grandpapa."

"You'll be going home before that," he said. "We leave in two weeks, as soon as Congress adjourns."

Oh, how I envied Nelly.

From my place in the hall I peeked at the general. He was older now, his face lined, his hair, which he still wore tied back in military fashion, near white. It was a kindly face. I'd never known him to be anything else but a kindly man.

He would hate me now. He would say I

was a bold little piece, full of ingratitude.

My vitals ached. I did not wish to hurt him. He was more of a father to me than my real one was.

And Lady Washington. Oh, she'd been part older sister and part mother to me. I knew her every wish, her every need. She turned to me when Nelly or Wash upset her. I knew her secret fears and anxieties.

She had just recovered from a bout of malaria. I worried for her. Who would make her tea the way she liked it, and put a vinegar-soaked napkin on her forehead if she again got headaches? She would look for me and I would not be there.

And then I heard Snipe calling from the back parlor, "The right thing, the right thing." I rushed to cover him. He'd over-heard the conversation between me and Hercules. Oh, I must cover him for the last time. For this night I was leaving!

The wharves of Philadelphia in early morning, or any time, were not a good place for a young girl, but Louise and Absalom were with me. They knew their way around. I bowed my head and kept my eyes to the ground as we passed the husky men loading the ships; the vendors selling them coffee, roasted corn, sausages, and cakes; the wealthy merchants just coming out of the coffeehouses to cast an eye to their cargo as it was being loaded; and the ships' masters inspecting the manifests as goods were loaded onto their tall-masted ships.

It was coming on to dayclean. In the east there was a red-streaked promise. The water would soon be sunlit. I'd lain awake most of the night waiting for the cock's crow, as Louise had directed. Then pattered, shoe-less, down three flights of stairs. I did not have to dress. I had never undressed for bed.

In the kitchen the only one I met was Christopher, up a good hour before anyone in the house to have his morning repast and heat the general's shaving water.

We hugged quickly. I ran inside to uncover Snipe for the morning. "Right thing," he squawked. "Right thing." I patted Frisk and gave him a bit of bread, hugged Christopher again, and I was gone.

Christopher had promised he would tell both the general and Lady Washington that I'd slipped out to buy fresh buns from the nearby bakery, if they discovered me gone. That would give me an extra three quarters of an hour.

The *Nancy* sailed with the tide. Six thirty. The morning was half amber and half rose colored now. Sun rays backlit the masts of the anchored ships, and gulls floated freely overhead, crying, as Absalom went out of his way to engage Captain Bowles in conversation. Louise and I tarried behind a pile of crates.

She nudged me. "There he is. Captain Bowles." He wore a black frock coat and breeches, a silk stock around his neck, and his hair, under the black tricorn, reached below his ears.

"He's a kindly man," Louise whispered. "But he won't discover you are aboard until this afternoon. Absalom will distract him, then you'll slip aboard. That's the way he wants it."

Captain Bowles walked right by the pile of crates, a few feet from us. We waited a minute, then Absalom led him a bit away. Louise threw a blanket over my head so that I looked like an old woman with a shawl, and we walked decorously to the gangway.

There, more crates hid me from view as I hugged her quickly.

"Go with God," she said.

As she released me a rough-looking seaman picked me up, flung me over his shoulder, and tramped up the gangway. I clung to him fiercely.

"Hold on, lassie," he said. "I'll have ye in the hold in a minute."

And I thought, *Well, mayhap he is God after all.* Because I knew that once he'd picked me up and lifted my feet from that gangway, I was free.

For what seemed like hours I lay cramped in the tiny space given me in the hold. Above my head I heard rough footsteps, men's shouts, and the captain's orders:

"Ready and about!" And, "Helm's hard alee!" And, "Haul taut the port jib and stay-sail sheets!"

We were moving!

I blinked. Except for a small glimmer of daylight in the hatch above me, I was in the dark. And every which way I moved, I felt something uncomfortable under me. And I smelled leather.

Saddles, I thought. *And harnesses. And Lord knows what else.*

But we were moving!

I was leaving Philadelphia!

I was free!

Louise and Absalom had made arrangements for me to board with a Negro family in Portsmouth. I would make my own living by sewing. I would indeed become a mistress of the needle.

How long had it been now since I'd left the president's house? Hours, it seemed. I was hungry. There had been no time for breakfast.

There now Lady Washington would be rising. Calling for me. "Oney, I want the black watered silk this morning. I must pay calls this day. Oney? Oney, where are you?"

The general would be finished with his letter writing, and shaving. Austin would be readying platters of ham and fresh fish for the breakfast table.

I dozed. How long, I do not know. But I awoke as the hatch above my head was opened and some vittles handed down. No fresh fish or bacon. No hoecakes and honey. Just bread, cheese, and a tin mug of coffee.

"Eat, lassie. What be your name?"

"Oney," I said. That was all. No last name. Just Oney.

"Eat and rest. The captain will be by later this day. When he comes, it must be that he just discovered you are a stowaway. He'll scold. Don't take it to heart. We're all actin' our parts. Always do."

"Are we out of Philadelphia?"

"We've cleared the harbor. Here" — he threw down another blanket — "put this under your head."

I thanked him. I ate in the dark. The bread

was fresh, the cheese good, the coffee like a brew of the gods.

Nelly would be coming into the dining room by now, asking if she could go and see Maria Morris. Christopher would just be appearing behind the general's chair in the dining room, in his red-and-white livery, to hold the chair out for him while the general sat down to breakfast.

"I don't know where that Oney is this morning," Lady Washington would be saying. "I called her and called her."

"You must be more severe with her," the general would say.

"She told me earlier that she was going to the bakery for fresh buns," Christopher would tell them.

I finished my breakfast. Would they care that I was gone? Would they talk about me afterward? Would the general say I had betrayed them? Would they remember me?

At Mount Vernon the mist would still be hovering over the river and the bottom-lands. The new spring lambs would be running about the pasture. The Persian jasmine, guelder rose, and linden trees would be blooming. The beans would be ready. The corn would already be growing high. Nathan would be starting the breakfast in the kitchen. The house servants would be coming from the covered walkway to the house.

I rolled up the blanket and put it under my head.

I thought of the day when I was three, when Mama grabbed my hand and dragged me to the front slope of the mansion house, then put her hand on the back of my neck, the way you hold a chicken just before you're about to chop its head off.

I could still hear her saying it. "You see that house, Oney Judge? Do you?"

I see it, Mama, I thought to myself. *I have always seen it. And I will always see it. And no, I won't ever be a hoe Negro. And I won't ever work in it again, either. Or any other house for a white master. Because now I am free.*

I am one of the Gone.

I slept.

AUTHOR'S NOTE

Oney Judge (sometimes called Ona) success-
fully fled to Portsmouth, New Hampshire, on
the *Nancy*, the ship owned by Captain John
Bowles of that town. Whether Bowles real-
ized he was carrying the favored slave of
Martha Washington, wife of the president of
the United States, is not known. It is most
likely, since he apparently gave passage to
many Negroes fleeing farther north, that he
did not know the slave in question belonged
to the president. He was in a risky business
anyway, transporting runaways. In slave
states they were considered stolen property,
and many slave states pronounced a sentence
of death for those who absconded with them.

When she reached Portsmouth, Oney
earned her own living as "mistress of her
needle." She lived with a free black family.

But there is no doubt that her life was def-
initely changed and more difficult. She
probably occupied one room. There were

no more pretty clothes, no more luxurious surroundings, old friends, important personages coming to visit, or excitement of living in the house of the president of the United States.

Oney Judge gladly gave up such creature comforts for her freedom.

When President and Mrs. Washington discovered her disappearance, there was much anguish in the household. It is a known fact that Martha Washington shed many tears for the little girl she had brought up and considered a member of her own family.

President Washington was, however, in a predicament. As president, as commander in chief and war hero, he was looked up to by everyone. Everything he did was scrutinized. He could not actively seek a runaway slave. So he contacted Joseph Whipple, collector of the port in Portsmouth, to help him find Oney. She had been seen walking the streets of the town by Betsy Langdon, daughter of Senator John Langdon, who had frequently visited the president's house in Philadelphia.

But Oney would not respond to any hello from Betsy Langdon in Portsmouth. By now it was late fall of 1796. The Washingtons had returned from Mount Vernon to Philadelphia.

Washington asked Joseph Whipple to have Oney seized in Portsmouth, put on a vessel, and sent to either Philadelphia or Alexandria.

Joseph Whipple set out to find Oney Judge and did. Indeed, he had an interview with her. But he was so taken with her character and her "thirst for complete freedom," that he wrote to Washington's secretary of the treasury, Oliver Wolcott Jr., "She expressed great affection and reverence for her master and mistress, and without hesitation declared her willingness to return and to serve with fidelity during the lives of the President and his lady if she could be freed on their decease."

Oney Judge wanted to negotiate with the president of the United States! He, of course, would not negotiate with her.

He wrote again to Whipple, very annoyed. He asked Whipple to try to have her sent back again. "To enter into such a compromise with her," he wrote, "as she suggested to you, is totally inadmissible, for reasons that must strike at first view; for however well disposed I might be to a gradual abolition, or even to an entire emancipation of that description of People, it would neither be politic or just to reward unfaithfulness with a premature preference; and thereby discontent beforehand the minds of all her fellow servants who, by their steady attachments, are far more deserving than herself of favor."

Washington furthermore said he would rather let Oney get away than provoke a public outcry. He was aware of his precarious position as president of the United States and the conduct he must follow.

So Oney Judge was not returned. A short time thereafter she met a free black man by the name of Jack Staines. She married him, and they had three children: Eliza, Nancy, and William. The marriage was happy, but Jack Staines died in 1803, leaving Oney to fend for herself and her children.

She accepted a job as a maid in the household of the Bartlett family in Portsmouth, and there she stayed until her children grew to adulthood. Her daughters, Nancy and Eliza, worked as maids when grown, to help support their mother. Her son left home to become a sailor, and whether lost at sea or not (nobody knows), he never came home again.

Oney's daughters died before she did. When Washington made a last attempt to retrieve her after she was married, she fled temporarily to the town of Greenland to live with a family named Jacks. After her husband died, she moved back there. When she could pull her weight no more in the Jacks's home, she became very poor, and people in Greenland made frequent donations to keep her comfortable. No doubt she had some celebrity there, being known as the free black woman who had once not only known, but lived with, the famous George Washington and his wife.

She died in February 1848.

As with all my historical novels, some of the characters in this book are invented, but most actually lived.

Hercules the cook, Nathan, Christopher, Betsy (Oney's mother), Myrtilla, Sambo Anderson, Lame Alice, One-Handed Charles, Austin, Billy Lee, and Charlotte are just some of the slaves who actually lived on Mount Vernon at the time.

Hercules did sell slops from the president's kitchen in both New York and Philadelphia to make money. He did buy fancy clothes with the money and saunter up and down the streets, attracting attention and making friends who could later help him escape. Today we call it networking.

Hercules ran off in 1796 and was never found by Washington.

Christopher returned to Mount Vernon

with the Washingtons, married, and tried to run off again. But the plot was foiled. Washington discovered it and forgave Christopher, who stayed on and was at Washington's bedside, weeping, when Washington died in December 1799.

Sambo Anderson was a colorful character on Mount Vernon, a "saltwater Negro," the name given to the slaves who actually came across the sea from Africa. His face was carved with markings as I describe. He told the children stories of Africa. He was allowed to use a musket to hunt and sold his birds to the Washingtons to keep their larder full. After he was freed by Washington under the terms of his will, Anderson supported himself by continuing to hunt for wild game in the area and selling it to respectable families and to hotels in Alexandria.

Billy Lee is the most famous of George Washington's slaves. He appears in portraits of the Washington family by Edward Savage. Washington kept diaries for most of his life, with the exception of the war years. The first mention of Billy Lee appears in 1768, when he accompanied Washington on many journeys.

He was Washington's body servant, huntsman, and trusted companion for more than thirty years. He went all through the war with Washington, always at his side. And only after the war, when he was incapacitated from bad knees, did he start to drink. Every time old friends who had served in the war came to visit Mount Vernon, they always asked to see Billy Lee.

Washington allowed him to bring his free black wife to Mount Vernon after the war. His high standing in the Washington household was unquestioned. But when Washington died, Billy Lee was a crippled alcoholic, living as a shoemaker on Mount Vernon. He was freed in Washington's will but stayed at Mount Vernon. Washington left him a house and a pension of $150 a year (a lot of money in those days). He died about 1828.

A slave named James did drown in the millrace, in 1775. All the overseers and managers I used, most importantly Lund Washington, did serve Washington in these positions at these times. And the British captain Richard Graves did come to Mount Vernon as I have portrayed, bringing his sloop-of-war up the Potomac, demanding provisions and taking away a number of slaves, some of whom were later recovered after the Battle of Yorktown (October 1781).

At that time many slaves were exposed to

smallpox by the British in hopes of sending them over the American lines to infect the soldiers, but the slaves fled to the woods while the final days of the battle were being waged.

The slaves on Mount Vernon were allowed to go "nightwalking," and it was a matter of serious concern to Lund Washington. They were permitted not only to go to Alexandria and sell their wares of a Sunday morning, but to attend special sporting events such as the horse races in Alexandria. Many plantation owners of the time allowed these "favors." And the slaves who accompanied the Washingtons to New York and Philadelphia during his presidency were permitted to go to the theater, the circus, and other entertainments in these cities.

Because of a Pennsylvania law that provided that adult slaves would have to be freed by their masters six months after coming to Pennsylvania, Washington did rotate his slaves back and forth between that city and Mount Vernon. But when his presidency was over and he returned to Virginia, he "forgot" to take some slaves with him. It was his way of freeing them. History does not tell us how many or who they were.

History does tell us the family had a parrot named Snipe and a dog named Frisk in Philadelphia. When the time came to go back to Mount Vernon, Washington wrote: "On one side I am called upon to remember the parrot; on the other to remember the dog; for my own part I should not pine much if both were forgot."

But, stern man that he was, he was a caring patriarch. He took under his wing the support and responsibility not only of his stepchildren, Patsy and Jackie, but his stepgrandchildren, Eliza, Nelly, Patsy, and Wash. He also paid for the education of the son of his dear friend the Marquis de Lafayette, who came from France to fight with him in the war. He supported and guided the upbringing of many nieces and nephews as well.

There are some indications, from research at Mount Vernon, that the Mount Vernon slave community had its own spiritual leaders. It is suspected that the slaves attended nearby Baptist, Methodist, and Quaker congregations. But there are also indications that some slaves still practiced their African religions. Artifacts uncovered bear such witness. The carvings on many uncovered bones mark them as ceremonial in the African religion and give substance to the belief that the slaves at Dogue Run Farm practiced voodoo or conjuring.

Oney's friendship with Louise Sturgis in Philadelphia was not documented. Indeed, Louise is a made-up character. But Absalom Jones and his friend Richard Allen, who started the first black churches in that city, are real.

When Oney served her mistress in Philadelphia, she must have met someone who encouraged her to take her freedom, who made the connection with Captain John Bowles, who really existed and made the run between Portsmouth and Philadelphia. Since we are told that she met many black people who were for freedom, I created Louise to help her.

Philadelphia was, at that time, very progressive in the abolitionist movement. This was the Age of Enlightenment. Philadelphia was a haven for free people of color. The Pennsylvania Abolition Society was very active. Dr. Benjamin Rush, a signer of the Declaration of Independence and a leading physician at the time, was an avid member, and he did help finance the first black church.

In the terribly hot summer of 1793 there was a horrible outbreak of yellow fever in Philadelphia that killed five thousand people. Dr. Rush, thinking that blacks were immune, appealed to them for help, and they came forward gladly. Many of those who died of the disease were Negroes who had picked up and buried the dead after caring for them in their homes when they were abandoned.

WRITINGS OF GEORGE WASHINGTON ABOUT SLAVERY

To Robert Morris, April 12, 1786
"There is not a man living who wishes more sincerely than I do to see a plan adopted for the abolition of [slavery]; but there is only one proper and effectual mode by which it can be accomplished, and that is by Legislative authority; and this, as far as my suffrage will go, shall never be wanting."

To John Francis Mercer, September 9, 1786
"I never mean to possess another slave by purchase; it being among my first wishes to see some plan adopted by which slavery in this country may be abolished by slow, sure, and imperceptible degrees."

To Marquis de Lafayette, April 5, 1785
"The scheme, my dear Marqs. which you propose as a precedent, to en-

courage the emancipation of the black people of this Country from that state of Bondage in wch. they are held, is a striking evidence of the benevolence of your Heart. I shall be happy to join you in so laudable a work."

From his will, July 9, 1799

"And whereas among those who will receive freedom according to this devise, there may be some who from old age or bodily infirmities, and others who on account of their infancy, that will be unable to support themselves; it is my Will and desire that all who come under the first and second description shall be comfortably cloathed and fed by my heirs while they live; and that such of the latter description as have no parents living, or if living are unable, or unwilling to provide for them, shall be bound by the Court until they shall arrive at the age of twenty five years; and in cases where no record can be produced, whereby their ages can be ascertained, the judgment of the Court upon its own view of the subject, shall be adequate and final.

"The Negroes thus bound, are (by their Masters or Mistresses) to be taught to read and write; and to be brought up to some useful occupation, agreeably to the Laws of the Commonwealth of Virginia, providing for the support of Orphan and other poor Children.

"I do, moreover, most pointedly, and most solemnly, enjoin it upon my Executors hereafter named, or the Survivors of them, to see that this cause respecting Slaves, and every part thereof be religiously fulfilled at the Epoch at which it is directed to take place; without evasion, neglect or delay, after the Crops which may then be on the ground are harvested, particularly as it respects aged, and infirm; seeing that a regular and permanent fund be established for their support so long as there are subjects requiring it; not trusting to the uncertain provision to be made by individuals."

Freedom for William (Billy) Lee

"To my Mulatto man William (calling himself William Lee) I give immediate freedom; or if he should prefer it (on account of the accidents which have befallen him, and which have rendered him incapable of walking or of any active employment) to remain in the situation he

269

now is, it shall be optional in him to do so. In either case however, I allow him an annuity of thirty dollars during his natural life, which shall be independent of victuals and cloathes he has been accustomed to receive, if he chuses the last alternative; but in full, with his freedom, if he prefers the first; and this I give him as a testimony of my sense of his attachment to me, and for his faithful services during the Revolutionary War."

To Frederick Kitt (Washington's former household steward in Philadelphia), from Mount Vernon, January 10, 1798

"We have never heard of Hercules our Cook since he left this place; but little doubt remains in my mind of his having gone to Philadelphia, and may yet be found there, if proper measures were employed to discover (unsuspectedly, so as not to alarm him), where his haunts are.

"If you could accomplish this for me, it would render me an acceptable service as I neither have, nor can get a good cook to hire, and am disinclined to hold another slave by purchase."

Oliver Wolcott Jr., September 1, 1796, re-

questing that Wolcott look into reports that runaway Oney Judge was seen in Portsmouth, New Hampshire

"Dear Sir: Enclosed is the name and description of the girl I mention to you last night. She has been the particular attendant on Mrs. Washington since she was ten years old; and was handy and useful to her being perfect Mistress of her needle.

"Whether she is stationary at Portsmouth or was there *en passant* only, is uncertain; but as it is the last we have heard of her, I would thank you for writing to the Collector of that Port, and him for his endeavours to recover and send her back. . . .

"I am sorry to give you, or any one else trouble on such a trifling occasion, but the ingratitude of the girl, who was brought up and treated more like a child than a servant (and Mrs. Washington's desire to recover her) ought not to escape with impunity if it can be avoided."

BIBLIOGRAPHY

Boyce, Burke. *Man from Mount Vernon.* New York: Harper and Brothers, 1961.

Dalzell, Robert F., Jr., and Lee Baldwin Dalzell. *George Washington's Mount Vernon: At Home in Revolutionary America.* New York: Oxford University Press, 1998.

Ferling, John E. *The First of Men: The Life of George Washington.* Knoxville, Tenn.: University of Tennessee Press, 1988.

Flexner, James Thomas. *Washington: The Indispensable Man.* Boston: Little, Brown, 1969.

Hirschfeld, Fritz. *George Washington and Slavery: A Documentary Portrayal.* Columbia, Mo.: University of Missouri Press, 1997.

Johnson, Charles, Patricia Smith, and the WGBH Series Research Team. *Africans in America: America's Journey through Slavery.* New York: Harcourt Brace, 1998.

Pinckney, Roger. *Blue Roots: African-*

American Folk Magic of the Gullah People. St. Paul: Llewellyn Publications, 1998.

Raboteau, Albert J. *Slave Religion: The "Invisible Institution" in the Antebellum South.* New York: Oxford University Press, 1978.

Randall, Willard Stearne. *George Washington: A Life.* New York: Henry Holt, 1997.

St. John, Jeffrey. *Forge of Union, Anvil of Liberty: A Correspondent's Report on the First Federal Elections, the First Federal Congress and the Creation of the Bill of Rights.* Ottawa, Ill.: Jameson Books, 1992.

Thane, Elswyth. *Potomac Squire.* New York: Duell, Sloan and Pearce, 1963.

SECONDARY SOURCES

Gerson, Evelyn. "Ona Judge Staines: Escape from Washington." June 2000. Online article at http://www.seacoastnh.com/blackhistory/ona.html.

Granley, Norma. *A Certain Species of Property Which I Possess: George Washington as a Slaveholder.* Northern Virginia Heritage, 1985.

Hayward, Nancy E., Mary V. Thompson, and Esther White. *Features in Footsteps: African American History.* A Cobblestone Publication, November/December 2000.

Mount Vernon Ladies' Association. *Slavery at Mount Vernon,* 1993.

Pogue, Dennis J. "The Archaeology of Plantation Life: Another Perspective on George Washington's Mount Vernon." *Virginia Cavalcade* 42, no. 2 (Autumn 1991).

Thompson, Mary V. "And Procure for Themselves a Few Amenities: The Private Life of George Washington's Slaves." *Vir-*

ginia Cavalcade (Autumn 1999).

Thompson, Mary, and Jennie Saxon. "George Washington's Plantation Bound by Slave History." 3 February 2001. Online article available at http://www. mountvernon.org/press/ 200lslavery.asp.

ABOUT THE AUTHOR

Ann Rinaldi is acclaimed for her historical novels, eight of which have been named Best Books for Young Adults by the American Library Association. Author of more than thirty titles, she sets the standard for the genre in excellence and accuracy with her modern-day classics *Wolf by the Ears* and *In My Father's House*. She lives in New Jersey with her husband.

The employees of Thorndike Press hope you have enjoyed this Large Print book. All our Thorndike and Wheeler Large Print titles are designed for easy reading, and all our books are made to last. Other Thorndike Press Large Print books are available at your library, through selected bookstores, or directly from us.

For information about titles, please call:

(800) 223-1244

or visit our Web site at:

www.gale.com/thorndike
www.gale.com/wheeler

To share your comments, please write:

Publisher
Thorndike Press
295 Kennedy Memorial Drive
Waterville, ME   04901